Accidental Awakening

Guardians Book 1

Damien Benoit-Ledoux

DBL Books / Purple Spekter™ LLP | Press

ACCIDENTAL AWAKENING | The Guardians Series | Part of the Spekter Superhero Universe™

KDP Paperback ISBN-13: 9781980949367

Kindle ASIN: B0799B6KWM

Work of Fiction

This story is a work of fiction. Names, characters, places, and incidents are the product of the author's imagination or are used fictitiously. Any resemblance to actual persons, living or dead, events, or locales is entirely coincidental.

Editions

Paperback

- 2.1 | November 18, 2020 | Updated Cover & Fonts
- 2.0 | December 11, 2019 | Professional Edits
- 1.2 | April 28, 2018 | Paperback Publication

Kindle

- 2.1 | November 18, 2020 | Updated Cover
- 2.0 | December 11, 2019 | Professional Edits
- 1.2 | April 28, 2018 | Updates with Paperback Publication
- 1.1| March 8, 2018 | Initial Typo Corrections
- 1.0 | March 3, 2018 | Kindle Launch

Contents

Book 1: Accidental Awakening is dedicated to Ron St. Germain, my personal superhero mentor, without whom I would not have found the characters and super powers to tell this awesome story.

The *Guardians* series is dedicated to all LGBTQ youth and young adults everywhere who have struggled to love themselves, or struggle to love themselves today.

Author's Notes

On Chronology

I believe you may be accustomed to reading the chapters of a book in order with the expectation that each chapter chronologically moves the story forward toward its climax and resolution. That being said: most of the time, Quinn's and Blake's story lines run in parallel chronology, but occasionally, a subchapter may take place at a different point in time. When it matters, I've been explicit about it. Otherwise, it doesn't matter.

On the *Guardians* Series Novels and Cliffhangers

Although this book has an ending, it is part of a larger work and isn't meant to stand alone. Thus, I've decided the book has a sufficient ending many would consider a cliffhanger ending.

To be more unclear: My writing style is inspired by the J. R. R. Tolkien sense of a book series. The primary books are not separate books only related by a series or collection, but rather the characters and stories in each book are part of a larger story that spans several novels.

On Making these Superheroes More Enjoyable

Let's be honest for a moment: extra stuff can be cool. That's why I created free bonus content for you to enjoy on my Web site about the **Guardians** series. It contains additional details about characters (spoiler free) and the unique places Quinn and Blake visit, such as the Orgonon Reactor Core.

You can access it here: worldanvil.com/w/the-spekter-superhero-universe-damientronus

Prologue

Quinn

My name is Quinton McAlester—known to the world as Blue Spekter—but my friends call me Quinn. I'm sixteen years old and I'm a superhero—and I love it!

Wait…

I know what you're about to ask me. You want to know if I can fly, if I'm bulletproof, if I'm faster than a speeding bullet, if I can bend metal or climb tall buildings. The truth is, I'm not like any *one* superhero you've read about in comics or seen in the movies. I'm something…different. I guess you could say I lucked out with my superpowers, but I'm getting ahead of myself. (I actually can't sling webbing around like Spidey, that would be really cool, though.)

I'm not the only one with superpowers; my best friend, Blake Hargreaves, got his superpowers the same way I did. (I'll get there, I promise.) Unlike your friendly neighborhood Spider-man, the Batman, or Wonder Woman, we don't live in a big city like New York or Gotham. We live in boring old Portsmouth, New Hampshire, where almost nothing happens except bad nor'easters and night crimes—but don't tell the locals I said it's boring. In truth, it's not. There's a lot going on, and the downtown traffic might make you think you're stuck on the Zakim Bridge in Boston, but it's no big city.

My family isn't very…normal…at least, what people around here think of as normal. See, I have two dads who are embarrassingly in love with each other. I know I should be grateful, but when you're my age, you don't appreciate the PDA of your parents, at all.

I talked about my friends earlier; there's Keegan, the boy I really like, but I don't think he knows I exist. Although Keegan isn't in my circle of friends yet, I'm working on that…big time. My other friends include Loren Davis, one of my English literature buddies, and Ravone Timber, who has a major crush on Blake. I'm not really sure how we became friends because she's so different from us, but she's part of our inner circle and I wouldn't have it any other way. There are a few others, but for brevity, last but not least there's Mr. St. Germain, my favorite science teacher. He's stupidly smart and really into superhero stuff, like from the comic books. That's why Blake and I trusted him to help us learn about our superpowers, because when things started happening, we couldn't figure out what the heck was going on—let alone now that we could control them.

Unfortunately, I have some enemies, too, and I don't really know why. Darien James is the biggest jerk and the stereotypical school bully. He is the Flash Thompson to my Peter Parker. He doesn't usually bug Blake, but he sure likes to pick on me. I think it's because I'm gay, but I'm not out—at least, I wasn't—when he started picking on me, so who knows what got his underwear in a twist.

So, while we don't live in a big city, there's enough going on to keep us busy, and by busy, I'm talking about school, track, homework, and work. Blake and I attend Portsmouth High School (Go Clippers!) and we're both on the track team. Our story starts at the beginning of our junior year. We both want to go to the same college after we graduate. I want to major in English, date cute boys, and then get an MFA in creative writing because I want to be a novelist. Blake doesn't have a specific dream or major yet, but he knows he wants to make a lot of money and be in charge of something big.

On nights and weekends, we both work as baristas at the local coffee shops: me at Breaking New Grounds, and Blake at Kaffee VonSolln. (Yeah, don't ask me how to pronounce it either.) It's fun because there's a natural, unspoken rivalry between the two shops, and our beloved residents and tourist fans are fiercely loyal to their brand of coffee, or *kaffee* as we like to mispronounce the word. Still, Blake and I don't care. Our parents let us keep the cash we earn (although mine make me save half of it for college), and we have fun with our classmates at the Fox Run Mall or the Regal Movie Theaters.

In the summers when we're not working, we hang around town at Prescott Park or drive into Maine to relax on the Ogunquit or York beaches. On weekends, we head north into New Hampshire or Maine to go camping with our friends or our families. Well, my family…Blake's parents are mean to him, and they treat him like crap. So, whenever he can, Blake likes to get out of the house and spend most of his time with me, my family, and a few of our close school friends. Speaking of camping, this is how my story gets started—on the weekend I went camping with my family and Blake up in Rangeley, Maine.

Shall we?

Blake

My name is Blake Hargreaves—known to the world as Dark Flame—a stupid name I absolutely *hate*. It's so friggin' pretentious. I loathe Hargreaves as well because my parents hate each other, and I'm stuck in the middle of their bullshit, forced to listen to them scream and yell at each other well into the night. Sometimes, I think they're just waiting for me to graduate high school before breaking up and getting a divorce. I wish they'd get it over with because it's not fun for me.

Money's tight, and though I work at one of the downtown coffee shops, I have to buy my own…everything. My parents rarely supply me with new clothes, and in the last two years I've grown a lot. I needed new shoes, underwear, pants, shirts…I had to pay for it all. Sometimes, Quinn McAlester, my best friend, chips in to help me, or his dads buy me stuff when they think I need it, but I hate taking their charity and their pity. However, I do love his family. Their home is peaceful, serene, and his dads are awesome together, if not a little too in love, if you catch my drift.

Oh, it's Quinn, by the way, who asked me to contribute to his little documentary project. So, I'm only doing this for him.

Still…

Quinn is really lucky, and it's hard not to be jealous of what he has. I just wish my mom and dad would…well, I already said it.

Quinn and I run track together at school, and we're gonna graduate from Portsmouth High in two years. We've talked about attending the same college, but we haven't really started looking yet. I don't know if we're going to be roommates or not, but I think it would be fun.

At least I did, before everything changed.

A while back, while camping with Quinn, my life changed forever. *Our* lives, I should say, since the thing happened to both of us. Mr. St. Germain, our nerdy science teacher, helped us figure out what happened when we decided to tell someone about the weird stuff that was happening to us.

Quinn loved it.

He had—and has—all these crazy ideas about helping and saving people, like he's going to become the next Superman or Invincible comic book hero. But in reality, people freak about this crap because they don't get it. To quote Carmine Falcone in *Batman Begins*, "You always fear what you don't understand."

Of course, Quinn's powers developed faster than mine, and they're different. I can't do all the things he can do yet, but some of the things I can do, I can do more powerfully than I let on. I don't think Quinn trusts me fully with our powers, and I resent him for thinking I'm less than capable of dealing with this. I think that's why he insists we do the superhero crap.

I don't mind helping him, but, I have my limits. If we get caught, our lives will irrevocably (today's vocabulary word challenge from English class) change forever. Our dreams—whatever they are—will be taken away from us by a bunch of pricks who will want to dissect us and figure out why we're so…uniquely powerful. I try to bring reason to his optimism, but I'm not succeeding. I fear he's gonna do more than just come out of the closet for being gay, he's gonna come out to the world as a Marvel class-five super freak.

I need to stop that from happening—no matter the cost—even if it means hurting my best friend.

Chapter 1

When Dreams Become Nightmares

Quinn

Quinn tried to speak, but the words caught in his throat and refused to leave his parched mouth and dry lips. Startled, he willed himself to cry out, but his voice failed him.

Indiscernible shouted words echoed around him, but he couldn't put them together or make sense of what was going on.

He felt unusually cold and realized he was lying on his back.

His eyelids were stuck shut, so he worked them open by wiggling the muscles around his eye sockets. A terrible bright blue light flashed in Quinn's eyes, and a searing pain blasted through his sixteen-year-old body as it inexplicably convulsed. He couldn't see what had happened, but he thought he had just been electrocuted. He felt hot and unusually agitated, like the time his finger slipped against the metal prong of a plug as he pushed it into the wall; electricity surged through his hand and left his fingers feeling numb and tingly at the same time.

Someone on his left—or so he thought—shouted.

Suddenly, his back spasmed and arched upward as his body reacted to another blast of hot pain tearing across his chest. This time, his eyes popped open, and he saw white lights in front...no, above him. At the same time, his lungs filled with air and his heart pounded in his chest.

"He's back," someone said.

Then, as mysteriously as he had awoken, everything went black.

The morning sun warmed and dried the beach sand as the ocean pulled away and approached low tide. Overhead, seagulls chirped and rode the rising thermals as they hunted for crabs and other low-surf delectables to feast on. Too many humans had fed bread and other foods to the scavengers, and as such, the birds tolerated the presence of humans on their beach far too well.

Quinn, lying on his back, propped himself up on his elbows and looked around Ogunquit Beach. To his left, morning joggers made their way up and down the beach. Older couples passed through their section of the beach, either hand in hand or chasing after one another as they joked and laughed. A young gay couple had set up their beach umbrella about twenty feet from him, and one of them applied sunscreen to their skin while the other found suitable music to play on their portable speaker. Behind him, the wave-ravaged sand dunes hosted tall grasses and nesting birds like the brown and white piping plover and the white and black least tern.

Quinn looked to his right and smiled. His boyfriend, Keegan, lay next to him on their shared multi-colored beach blanket. He was napping on his stomach; an intentionally placed T-shirt draped over his head kept it from burning in the hot sun. The sunscreen on his back and legs glistened in the sunlight and made Quinn smile.

You're so damn sexy, he thought. *I'll never know what I did to get you to notice me, but I'm so happy you did.*

An odd itch on his left arm drew his attention away from Keegan. When he tried to move his right hand to scratch his arm, he couldn't lift it from the beach blanket. Panic set in when he realized he couldn't move his ankles or his left hand either. They seemed to be restrained, but he couldn't tell how. A sharp prick in his left shoulder made him cry out.

"Keegan! Help me."

His boyfriend didn't move. Instead, the beach faded away into blackness.

Keegan, please…

Quinn's throat felt dry and scratchy again. Through his closed eyelids, the bright white light he saw told him the sun was probably overhead and he had fallen asleep on the beach.

Crap. Did I put on enough sunscreen?

He tried to raise his hand to shield his eyes, but something held his hand in place. He realized his wrists, ankles, and now his torso were still tied down.

What the heck?

He blinked in the bright sunlight and opened his eyes only to discover the bright afternoon sunlight came from a window to his right. He attempted to clear his throat but had no saliva to wet his mouth. He looked down and saw he was wearing a hospital gown. White hospital sheets covered him to his stomach, and the bed rails of his hospital bed were both raised.

"What?" he said in soft surprise, his scratchy voice barely above a whisper.

"You awake?" a familiar but also scratchy voice to his left asked. Quinn's head snapped left to look for the voice, but instead he saw the foot of an identical hospital bed on the other side of a beige curtain he wanted to pull back, but couldn't. The voice belonged to Blake Hargreaves, his best friend.

"I just called for Nadia. She'll be here in a second." Blake's voice sounded just as hoarse as his own.

"Who?"

"The nurse."

"Where are we?"

"The hospital."

"Why?"

"We got sick or something after we left that cave thing we discovered, remember? I woke up about an hour ago. Don't say too much about the cave thing though, the armed guards are just outside the door."

"The who?"

Quinn remained confused as the golden-oak-stained door on the other side of the room opened and a black Dominican woman in purple scrubs popped in. Her hair was tightly braided in rows from front to back and finished in a low bun at the base of her skull, just above the back of her neck.

"He's awake," Blake said.

"Oooh, this is good news, Mister Blake," a strong, accented voice said. She walked toward the foot of Quinn's bed and stopped, regarding him with a wide smile.

"Can you untie me now, please?" Blake asked.

"Greetings, Mister Quinn," the nurse said, ignoring Blake's question. She looked Quinn up and down, her face serious for a moment. Then she looked at something over his head and smiled again.

He looked up and saw a massive monitor over his head, displaying his vitals and other information.

"You are a very lucky, healthy young man today," she said, eyes darting across the monitor. "I am glad to see you have improved."

"Can you pull the curtain back, please?" Blake asked, his voice still scratchy.

"Yes, I can do that for you, Mister Blake." She pushed the curtain back toward the wall, removing the obstructed view between them. Quinn made eye contact with his best friend, who lifted his head from his pillow and winked at him.

Okay, so you look fine, but…

"Why am I tied up?" Quinn asked, his hoarse voice betraying panic.

"You were restrained for your safety when you were brought into the hospital."

"Why?"

She stopped looking at Blake's monitor and met Quinn's gaze. "My name is Nadia Nyongo. I have been your primary day nurse."

"Have been? How long have I…have we…been here? And why are we tied up?" Quinn watched as Blake plopped his head back on his pillow.

"That is not for me to tell you." Nadia discreetly rolled her eyes to Quinn's left, and he looked at the door. Two armed, muscular-looking guards in black clothes—who looked like they could be in the military—stared back at him. Each held some kind of rifle in their hands.

You've got to be kidding me.

"When Doctor Madison comes in, she will tell you what you need to know."

"I want to see my parents."

"Please, wait for the doctor, Mister Quinn," Nadia said. "I will tell her you are awake. She will tell you what you need to know."

"But I just want to—"

"Please, Mister Quinn," Nadia interrupted, raising her hands in surrender. "Let me get the doctor."

Quinn took a deep breath and glared at Nadia as she walked out of the room and shut the door behind her.

"Where the hell are we?" Quinn asked, looking at Blake.

"Fuck if I know. They told me I'd have to wait for you wake up. But the doctor's sorta cute, so there's that. Do you have to pee yet?"

"No, why?"

"Oh, well I did when I woke up. They made me use the duck."

"The what?" Quinn looked at his friend quizzically.

"That plastic thing," Blake said, nodding his head toward the portable men's urinal hanging on the side of his right railing. Quinn didn't see one hanging from his bed rail.

"Oh. Did you see those guards?"

"Yep."

"We're in some kind of special wing of the hospital, I bet," Quinn said. His mouth finally salivated, and he swallowed. "Like a secure wing or something."

Blake chuckled. "We watch too much TV."

"We have to be! We're being guarded. Do you know *anything* about what's going on?" Quinn asked his best friend.

"All I know is we're still in Rangeley. The doctor popped in about a half hour ago, but she told me she would talk with both of us when you woke up. And then there's the guards, the creepy guy in the black suit, and Nadia. And the nurse who helped me pee, who you'll probably think is cute."

Quinn chuckled. He knew at some point he'd have to pee, but he couldn't imagine why they wouldn't let him use the toilet. "So you don't know why we're tied up?"

"They said it's for our safety."

"Uh-huh," Quinn said, staring at the leather-and-cloth restraints on his wrists.

Someone knocked at the door, and it opened. A brown-haired middle-aged woman of modest height and weight, wearing heels that clacked on the laminate tile floor, a blue dress, and a white doctor's coat entered the room. A stethoscope hung from her neck, and a blue pen jutted out of her coat's right breast pocket. The words *Rangeley Medical* were embroidered on the left side of the jacket, but her ID badge—clipped to the lapel of the coat—had flipped backwards, preventing Quinn from seeing her name.

Nadia followed her into the room.

"Hi, Quinn. Glad to see you're awake."

"Finally, we can get some answers," Blake said. Quinn looked at his best friend with curiosity. Usually, Blake's short temper caused him to fly off the handle in anger, but Quinn felt more impatient than his friend seemed. Maybe whatever was in the IV bags they were hooked up to mellowed him out.

"Why are we here?" Quinn asked. "What's going on?"

The doctor smiled. "I'm sure you both have lots of questions. My name is Doctor Amy Madison. I've been in charge of your care since you arrived on Sunday."

"What day is it?"

"Today is Thursday. Do you boys know where you were this weekend?"

We've been here almost all week?

Blake answered the doctor. "Yeah, we were camping with his family at the Wood Lakes Campground on Quimby Pond."

Dr. Madison studied him for a moment and nodded. "That's right. At some point on Sunday morning, you were found by campers or hikers outside the campground. Both of you were unconscious and were transported here by ambulance. Shortly after you arrived at the hospital's emergency room, you both went into cardiac arrest. We were able to resuscitate you, but it wasn't easy. When your hearts stopped, we had to defibrillate you. The first time, something unusual happened."

"Like?" Quinn asked. *The emergency room?*

"Oddly, you both went into cardiac arrest within seconds of each other. Two different sets of emergency room doctors worked on each of you. That's a miracle in itself, given the time of day and the small staff we have here. Two different sets of equipment were used to defibrillate and save your lives."

What the hell happened to us?

"That doesn't sound strange," Blake commented. "I mean, outside of why we're here and all."

"This is where it becomes unusual. As a complete coincidence, the decision to jumpstart your hearts was made at nearly the same moment, again, by two different doctors in two different rooms. One of those doctors was me. Nurses charged the defibrillators simultaneously, and by random happenstance, the other doctor and I called the same countdown. When the defibrillators fired, a bright blast of energy exploded between the two of you."

Quinn and Blake looked at each other and then looked back at the doctor.

She used her hands to gesture an explosion and tapped her chest. "You each discharged a bright white light from the center of your torso when the paddles tried to restart your heart. From my perspective, it traveled through the wall separating you. We don't know what it was or why it happened, but it did not happen the second time, when we finally managed to restart your hearts at slightly different moments."

"So why does my throat hurt?" Quinn asked. His brain struggled to process what sounded like a scene from a science fiction medical thriller.

"We had to intubate you to help you breathe. We can't explain why, but you both had a hard time breathing. That shouldn't have been the case in two sixteen-year-old boys. Incidentally, the tubes came out this morning. That's why your voices sound a little scratchy, and your throats might be a little sore. You were hooked up to life support."

"You've got to be kidding me!" Blake exclaimed.

"I wish I was."

"So where are my parents?" Quinn asked.

"Both sets of parents are in town, but they're not allowed to see you yet. You've been isolated for study."

"Why?" the boys asked simultaneously.

"Well, the exploding white light for starters. Then, strange things happened while you were unconscious. Quinn, things around you moved on their own. Blake, the temperature on your side of the room inexplicably fluctuated between cold and hot.

"We reached out to the Wilhelm Reich Museum to see if anything odd was going on—"

"The what?" Blake asked, looking at Quinn.

"I've never heard of that either," Quinn commented.

"It's a home that's been converted into a museum. It's also home to the Orgone Energy Institute. The campground you were staying at is about a mile east of the museum."

Quinn became suspicious of the story. "Why would you reach out to a museum?"

"Well, they, uh—"

"Thank you, Doctor Madison, that will be enough," a man in a black suit standing in the doorway said.

That must be the creepy guy Blake mentioned.

Dr. Madison turned her head and nodded at the man. Then she smiled at Blake and Quinn. "Just rest up and cooperate, and we'll have you out of here in no time." She winked and stepped back.

Cooperate?

Nadia nodded her head. She walked around the bed and set Quinn's call button within reach of his hand. "You can press this if you need anything, okay, Mister Quinn?"

"I need my dads," Quinn said, glaring at the nurse and the doctor.

"Very soon, I promise," Nadia responded. Then she winked at him and followed the doctor out of the room.

The man in the suit stepped into their room and shut the door behind him. He pulled a chair from the side of the room, set it between their beds, unbuttoned his jacket, and sat down.

Quinn studied his face. It was youthful, but firm—full of responsibility and stress. The man's medium-length black hair was parted from the left and styled with a shiny hair gel. Although the man had shaved, Quinn could see the stubble of a mustache, soul patch, and chin strap beard. His face structure had sharp features like a male model, and Quinn felt oddly smitten with the handsome man, even though his instincts warned him to be cautious.

"Gentlemen, it's good to see you, uh, awake."

"Who are you?" Blake asked.

"My name is Victor Kraze. I represent a concerned group of individuals who are interested in what happened to you this weekend."

"Are you responsible for keeping our parents away from us?"

"Yes, I am," he said flatly, nodding.

"Why? Do they know we're awake?"

"When Dr. Madison called us, it became critical to place you in isolated observation. Your situation is unique. And yes, your parents have been informed of your progress. They know you've regained consciousness. Quinn, your dads were obviously already here in Rangeley. Blake, your parents arrived on Monday, I believe."

"They didn't even come up on Sunday when this happened?" Blake asked softly. Quinn sensed his friend's disappointment with his parents' apathy.

"I'm not sure your parents could have made the trip, Blake," Victor said.

"Right," Blake said softly.

Quinn sighed. Blake's parents were alcoholics, and they were probably half in the bag when they got the call. "Do they know we're tied up like prisoners or crazy people?" he asked.

Victor slightly tilted his head to the left. "I'm not at liberty to say right now. How about we make a deal? You give me something I want, and I'll give you something you want."

Quinn and Blake looked at each other, confused.

"What do you want?" Quinn asked. "This feels like a superhero cartoon where you play out to be the villain in disguise."

Victor smirked. "Then it's a good thing I don't have evil superpowers"—he leaned forward—"or do I?" His face became serious again, and he sat back. "Information. I want you to tell me everything you did this weekend, beginning with waking up on Friday morning."

"That's it?" Blake asked.

"That's it," Victor answered, smiling. "Pretty easy, right?"

"Who do you work for again?" Quinn asked, hoping to catch Victor off guard.

The corner of Victor's lip curled upward before he answered. "I represent a concerned group of individuals who are interested in what happened to you this past weekend at the campground and here at the hospital."

Right.

Quinn, accepting defeat, looked at Blake and shrugged. The boys proceeded to tell Victor what he wanted to know.

Chapter 2

Junior Year at Portsmouth High

Quinn

Quinn blinked his blue eyes in the morning light and yawned. He stretched and then rolled over, refusing to get up despite the bright sunlight shining in his eyes. It was probably seven o'clock, but he didn't care. The fact that school started before Labor Day sucked, but the number of snow days in New Hampshire forced the school system to expand the school year on the front and back ends.

A knock at the door startled him. "Time to get up, son," one of his dads said through the closed door. It was Aren, whom he called Daddio.

"Yup," he called out, burying his head under the covers.

Ugh, he thought. *Let's get this morning thing over with.*

He threw the covers off, rotated himself to a sitting position, and put his feet on the carpeted floor. His toes gripped the carpet as he stretched his hands and arms high above his head and then stood up. Then he slapped himself in the face a couple of times to wake up and fell forward to the floor and started cranking out pushups.

One, two, three!

At fifty, he flipped over and worked through one hundred crunches.

Ninety-seven, ninety-eight, ninety-nine, one hundred.

He collapsed to the floor, his breath momentarily sucked out of him as his abs burned good after his early morning workout.

"Quinn, you up?" his other dad, Tim—whom he called Dad—asked through the door.

"Yep!" he answered.

"Okay."

Quinn pulled himself off the floor and flexed in the mirror over his dresser. His abs were on point and his chest had a nice pump to it. He chuckled when he saw how wild his long, wavy, dirty-blonde bed-head hair looked in the mirror. Then he quickly made his bed and grabbed his towel from behind his door and made his way to the bathroom across the hall.

When he had finished showering, he wrapped the towel around his waist and shaved. Around him, he heard the quiet sounds of his family's morning routine.

Daddio was downstairs in the kitchen, probably whipping up some eggs and turkey bacon for breakfast. Dad was in the shower and had probably already run five miles. He would have to leave for the law firm first, and he'd bring Quinn to school on the way. Daddio didn't have to be in the office at the small publishing company he owned until eight thirty, so he had time to get all the morning rituals done, like making breakfast and packing three lunches.

Quinn finished dressing and checked himself in the mirror, approving the cute outfit he had put together. He wore a short-sleeved blue-and-white gingham button-down shirt paired with gray shorts and navy-blue canvas shoes. It was still hot out, and he didn't want to sweat a lot.

After a few minutes, Quinn sat with his dads around the table and wolfed down some over-peppered scrambled eggs, turkey bacon, a banana, and a glass of orange juice. Dad was wearing one of his usual business suits, and Daddio wore some plaid boxers and tank top.

"Sorry about that," Daddio said. "The filter thing on the pepper popped off, and I tried to scoop out what I could."

"Thermodynamics, babe," Dad responded, smiling. Daddio grinned back at him.

Quinn rolled his eyes. His dads were fitness nuts, and they found ways to incorporate vitamin and nutritional hacks into their cooking. Thermodynamics pills, or fat burning pills, were basically shots of different kinds of pepper. Dad believed adding more pepper to your food saved tons of unnecessary spending on potentially bogus supplements—if you could handle the added heat and flavor.

"You excited for this weekend, Quinn?" Daddio asked.

Quinn nodded.

"I know I am," Dad commented. "Three days without the law firm emailing me will be glorious."

"Right," Quinn responded. "Unless you're going to turn off your cell phone, you're going to be on it."

"I won't, I swear. In fact, challenge accepted, Captain Needa," Dad said, sitting up and smiling.

"Not quite," Daddio quipped. Needa was the captain of the Star Destroyer *Avenger* in Star Wars. Darth Vader Force-choked him for losing and failing to capture the escaping *Millennium Falcon*. As an avid Star Wars fan, Daddio worked in Star Wars references whenever he could. When *Dad* did it, Quinn knew the stakes were high.

"I'll give you my phone. You can turn it off for me," Dad added.

"Don't fail me," Daddio answered in as deep a voice as he could muster. Then he mimicked Darth Vader's breathing. Quinn laughed.

Dad rolled his eyes and smiled. "My nerds."

"Oh, you love it too, babe," Daddio said.

Quinn shared a laugh with his dads and they finished their breakfast.

"You have practice after school, right?" Dad asked, pulling into the school parking lot.

"Yup."

"All right, well, have a great day and may the Force be with you."

Quinn chuckled and rolled his eyes. "You're so weird."

"You love it, Batman."

"You're out of control."

Dad stopped the car and smiled at his son. "Give us a hug."

Quinn leaned over and hugged his father. "See you tonight."

"Yep. Don't forget we have to finish packing for the weekend. Make sure Blake is ready to go in the morning, okay?"

"Will do, Dad," Quinn said, getting out of the car. He grabbed his backpack from the back seat and shut the door, waving to his dad as he turned and walked toward the high school's beige-and-red-brick main building.

"Aww, did ya get dropped off by your daddy, little boy?" Darien James asked. A few of his cronies, including Kyle and Tony, his loyal followers, laughed around him.

Quinn glared at him but continued walking. "They're my dads, not my daddies."

"Oh, well, I'm so sorry. Did you hear that guys? They're his *dads*, not his *daddies*," Darien repeated with a sing-songy, derogatory tone.

"Just keep walking," Blake said, catching up to him and grabbing Quinn's arm before the situation escalated. "It's only the third day of school, and they're not worth it."

"Maybe not," Quinn said, "but it would be great to punch his lights out one day."

"And then you'd get suspended or worse," Blake said, reminding him of the consequences of such an outburst.

"Yeah, that's right, take your little boyfriend away, Blakeypoo," Darien called after them through a fit of laughter.

Blake flipped him the bird, unbeknownst to Quinn.

"You rarely have to take that kind of crap from them," Quinn said. "Besides, they don't even know I'm gay."

"But I do, and it bothers me that they think they can treat you like that. What do you think will happen when you come out? Are they magically going to go away or stop? They shouldn't pick on you in the first place for any reason, let alone your sexuality."

"I guess."

"Besides, if one of us is gonna throw a punch, everyone expects me to do it. You, not so much."

Quinn looked hard at his friend. "I'm not a wimp."

"That's not what I meant," Blake said, slowing down. He turned to face Quinn. "You're just, you, know, the good guy. I'm the bad guy. I've got more demons and skeletons in my closet, and everyone knows it. It makes perfect sense for me to punch Darien's lights out for you."

"Maybe," Quinn said. "But if I do it, maybe people will pay attention and think about *why* I did it. 'What pushed the good kid to lose it and lash out on Darien?' they'll wonder."

"Sounds like every school shooting, to be honest. No one knows why the kid did it because no one was paying attention."

"You're getting deep," Quinn said, chuckling.

"No, I'm getting real."

"Uh-huh. So, how was your morning?"

Blake shrugged. "The usual, I guess. My dad was already up and out of the house when I got up, and my mom was still in bed, probably pissed off or passed out from last night or something. They got in some big fight about the grocery bill and I just...I tuned it out."

"Did they drink a lot again?" Quinn asked.

"Who knows. I didn't think about it when I picked up the empty beer cans from the living room carpet and the kitchen counter. Beer reeks when it's been sitting around all night."

"Oh," Quinn said. It wasn't a smell he was familiar with. "Did you eat some breakfast?"

"Yeah, Pop-Tarts, the breakfast of champions."

"Better than nothing, I guess," Quinn said with a shrug.

"If you say so. I can't wait to be out of there in two years and living on campus. It's time for a change, time to move on, time for bigger and better things for Blake."

"Hey, boys," Ravone Timber called out from a bench. "Come and sit a spell before hell."

"OMG, gurl, love your hair," Quinn said the minute his eyes set upon the red streak she had added to her normally brown hair. It matched the red leather jacket she wore over a white T-shirt and a well-fitted black skirt.

"Thank you, hot stuff. Love your outfit. And Blake…," Ravone said, eyeing Blake's standard outfit of blue jeans, faded dark blue Converse sneakers, and a T-shirt. "Roguishly handsome as usual."

"I try not to disappoint," he said, smiling. "The red streak in your hair is badass."

"What about me, you guys?" Loren Davis asked. He wore red Converse sneakers with black and white horizontal striped leggings that disappeared under a black leather skirt. On top, she wore a gray T-shirt with the words "Rock on, Queer."

Loren self-identified as genderqueer and used both he and she pronouns, thoroughly confusing the quaint folk of Portsmouth, an accepting East Coast city—but it was no Los Angeles.

"Tramp," Blake said.

"Slut," Quinn added.

"Wouldn't have it any other way," Loren said, smiling.

"Seriously, your outfit is fierce today," Quinn said. "I'm not sure I could pull it off."

"Don't," Loren said abruptly.

"Oh, okay," Quinn said, startled.

"It's my look and you can't have it," Loren added, winking at Quinn, who smiled.

"There goes Professor Xavier," Ravone said, nodding toward one of the teachers entering the building. *Professor Xavier* and *Mr. Spock* were two of the affectionate nicknames the students bestowed upon Mr. St. Germain, the high school's nerdiest science teacher. His penchant for all things science fiction came up often in class, and the students knew he could be easily pulled off topic with questions about the comic universes, Star Wars, Star Trek, and anything else both nerdy and geeky.

"Here comes your boy, shirtless as usual," Blake said, gently punching Quinn in the shoulder.

Quinn felt the blood rush to his face as he nervously swatted Blake's hand away. "Stop it, B."

"Aw, you're blushing," Ravone said.

"Too cute," Loren added.

"Guys, stop it," Quinn said, losing focus of everything around him as a shirtless Keegan Miller rolled closer on his longboard. That day, Keegan wore black sunglasses and wireless headphones on his head over his dirty-blonde hair, a white-and-blue-striped button-down shirt tied around his waist over black shorts, and dark gray skateboarding sneakers. He carried his backpack in his right hand. His tight abs flexed with every dip and push he made to propel himself forward.

"Are you gonna say something?" Ravone asked.

"He better," Blake said.

"Give him space, guys," Loren said. "But you better say something, just saying."

Twenty feet, fifteen feet, ten feet...

"Hi, Keegan," Quinn called out, his voice sounding a little higher than he liked. Keegan looked over briefly and nodded, barely raising a few fingers to wave as he whizzed by.

"Ouch," Blake said softly.

Quinn took a deep breath and sighed. His beautiful crush had once again passed him by. Nothing had changed over the summer, and Keegan, who was proudly out of the closet, hadn't shown any interest in dating anyone yet. Quinn hoped to change that, but as they started junior year, his time was running out; someone else might snag Keegan's heart first.

The first bell rang out, alerting the students it was time to come in. Near the school's entrance, Keegan pulled on his shirt, picked up his longboard, and ran into the building.

"Okay, let's go," Loren said. "There are things to accomplish before the 3:20 bell."

"Like what?" Ravone quipped.

"Learning," Loren said, drawing out the word. The group of friends began walking to the covered entrance of the school.

"And track practice," Quinn added.

"Well, for you guys. When school's out, I'm outta here for three days. Aren't you two going camping this weekend?" Loren asked.

"Yup," Quinn and Blake answered simultaneously.

"Well, if I don't see you later, have fun."

"We plan to," Quinn said, eyeing Blake.

His best friend smiled and nodded to him. "Yeah, it will be great to get away for a few days."

Chapter 3

Bullies and Distractions

Blake

Blake shifted in his seat during the last period of the day, which for him was English Lit, his best friend's favorite subject. The teacher had just finished handing out the reading list for the semester, which sucked. All of it sucked, and Blake didn't care. He desperately needed a change and a break from all of the bullshit in his family life.

"Mr. Hargreaves?"

"What?" Blake said, startled.

"Are you with us, young man?" Mrs. White, his English Literature teacher, asked.

"Yeah, sorry." He hated when teachers caught him daydreaming, but sometimes they droned on and on and his own worries crept out from the shadows of his mind."

"Perhaps you'd like to share with the class what's so much more inter—"

"No, I wouldn't," Blake snapped, making direct eye contact with Mrs. White. It was a bold move that could have been mistaken as threatening, but Blake gambled Mrs. White looked forward to the 3:20 bell as much as he did—although Blake would be able to take out his frustrations on the school's running track or the streets of Portsmouth.

"All right, then. Let's continue with the reading assignments, shall we?" Mrs. White said.

Thirty minutes later, Blake walked into the locker room to change into running shorts and a tank top with most of the team. The guys around him joked about this and that, but most were upset the coaches hadn't cancelled any of the practices before the long weekend.

Quinn rushed in and squeezed into the space between Blake and the next guy over. "Hey, what's up?"

"Just glad the day's over, you know?"

"Ugh, I know what you mean. I can't believe they gave us homework over the weekend. That's so obnoxious."

"I only got math and social studies homework."

"Yeah, but still."

Blake, Quinn, Darien, and the rest of the track team ambled onto the track field where Coach Tomlin was waiting for them.

"There are only two ways off this field, maggots. A pine box or a school bus," Coach Tomlin yelled. "The choice is yours."

Coach Tomlin, a man with a slightly hunched stature and a small gut, wore beige khaki shorts that sat too high on his waist and a tucked-in maroon Portsmouth High polo shirt. His pale legs disappeared into maroon crew socks and gray sneakers. White curls of hair spilled out from underneath the blue and yellow U.S. Navy ball cap he wore. As white as the Coach's hair seemed to be, fuzzy dark gray eyebrows hovered over the auto-tinting sunglasses that rested on the bridge of his nose.

"I know it's almost the weekend, but we can't stop. I need to make sure you're all fit as fiddles for next week's races. So get stretching, and in about fifteen minutes, you're all going to run the New Castle loop."

The boys groaned because the New Castle loop meant a nearly ten-mile run around Portsmouth through New Castle Island and then back to the high school. Most of the boys would run it in about seventy minutes, while others would take ninety minutes. Quinn started stretching and quickly texted his dad that he would not be free until five thirty that night.

"What are you doing?" Blake asked, looking at Quinn as he played with his phone.

"Texting my dad," Quinn said, "I need to let him know when to pick me up. Do you want him to pick you up as well?"

"Sure," Blake said, "that would be great. Would it be okay to sleep over your house tonight? I don't really want to be around my family if I don't have to right now. Even though it's Friday and I probably won't see them because they'll drink themselves into oblivion, I just—"

"Of course," Quinn said. "Are you packed?"

"Yeah," Blake said, "I did most of it last night. I just need to grab my bags and my sleeping bag. We're using your air mattress this time, right?"

"Yep," Quinn answered.

"Great. It's more comfortable than mine."

"All right, you maggots!" The retired navy-officer-turned-coach yelled, "Enough stretching, head on out! See you back in seventy minutes."

The boys groaned again, but they dutifully started running away from the school, their captain leading them on the run.

"I'm glad we don't have to get up early tomorrow," Blake said as he started running alongside Quinn.

"Well, that's not true. We have to leave the house by six, so—"

"Yeah, but I meant we don't have to go to school tomorrow. My legs are going to be so sore in the morning."

"Gotcha."

The heat and humidity of the late summer sun bore down on the track team as they ran across the narrow roads and bridges that carried them onto New Castle Island. Most of the boys had pulled off their shirts and tucked them into the waistbands of their running shorts. Sweat poured down Blake's face and torso as they rounded the tight curves of New Castle Island, narrowly dodging cars that slowed down to accommodate the entire Portsmouth High School boys' track team. At about the halfway point, they passed the girls' track team, running in the opposite direction. They waved and high-fived each other and continued on toward the school.

When they got back to the athletic fields, most of the guys collapsed onto the soft grass of the football field that was inside the running track. Coach Tomlin had set up Gatorade stations while they were out, and the boys eagerly sucked down as much Gatorade as they could to replenish their dehydrated bodies.

Most of the guys stretched, and Blake was no exception. As he sat on the grass watching the late guys return to the field, he saw Darien, Kyle, and Tony eyeing Quinn. Then, Darien walked over to Quinn and said something that made Quinn turn away in disgust. He watched Darien push Quinn, who spun around, slapping Darien's hand away from his body. Some of the other guys began to notice the commotion, and soon all eyes were watching Darien and Quinn.

Blake stood up and walked over. When he got close enough he could hear Darien teasing Quinn. When the word *faggot* came out of Darien's mouth, Blake's hands balled into fists and he angrily stormed up to Darien.

"What did I just hear you say?" Blake shouted, "Did you just call him a faggot?"

"I did, and what of it?" Darien asked, stepping back only to step forward again to correct his awkward flinch. "He is, you know." A wicked smile came across Darien's face. "I bet you'd know, given you're his best friend and all. Or maybe you're more than just best friends, huh, Blake?" Darien asked, jeering at him while Kyle and Tony snickered behind them.

You son-of-a-bitch.

"You don't know that," Blake said, "and it's none of your damn business how close of friends we are."

"That doesn't sound like a denial," Darien said.

"Who cares what it sounds like," Blake spat back, his anger boiling inside him. "Nobody cares about that shit anymore. Why should you?"

"No," Darien said. "That's not how it works. People *do* care about being around faggots like Quinn, and maybe you."

Some of the guys behind Blake started shaking their heads. A few of them started saying, "Knock it off," or "Back off, Darien." It was clear the team was split. Well, more than split. Only Darien and three of his friends shared the particularly hateful viewpoint.

Out of the corner of his eye, Blake saw Coach Tomlin approach, his face firm and telling that he knew a fight was about to break out. "You need to knock it off and back down," Blake said. "You have no right to treat him like shit."

"I have every right, and I don't need riffraff like you telling me what I should and shouldn't do," Darien spat.

Blake stepped back and cocked his right arm back, his hand tightening into a fist, ready to strike.

"Do it," Darien said, taunting him.

"Blake!" The coach yelled. "Think about your choices." Blake lowered his hand and took a deep breath, then bared his teeth, twisted his face with rage, and let loose a primal roar at Darien as his body tensed and his fingers curled into claw-like shapes.

Darien's eyes widened, and he stepped back in fear. "Holy shit," he said. "Easy, man, easy."

"Fuck off," Blake screamed.

"That's enough, Blake," Coach Tomlin said sternly. "Darien, take your friends and go shower. Get out of here. When you come back next week, I don't want to hear another word of this, is that clear?"

"Yes, Coach," Darien said, his fingers crossed behind his back.

Blake rolled his eyes in disgust.

"I dealt with this kind of crap in the Navy when I was on a battleship. I don't want to deal with this crap in a high school, is that understood? If I hear this kind of foulness from that feculent cesspool of a mouth you have, you're off the team, permanently."

"Yes, Coach," Darien said, looking at him funny. Then he turned and walked toward the locker rooms with his friends.

Blake smirked. Coach had a way of mixing in unexpected and strange Navy jargon—they assumed—with normal, everyday speech.

"All of you, listen up," Coach Tomlin barked, addressing the track team. He put his hands on his waist as the team turned to listen. Then, he pointed as he spoke. "None of you should have to deal with Darien's horse shit. I don't care if any of you are gay, so no one on this team says another word about another teammate liking boys, girls, or both. You all have the same damn hormones running through your bodies, so you're all dealing with similar stuff. Sure, the circumstances will be different for some of you, but puberty in high school is like being on this team. You're all in this together and you all help each other win, so cut the crap and grow up a little. Is that clear?" Coach asked. He returned his hands to his waist.

"Yes, sir," the team said together.

"No one's sexuality ever let them *win* or *not win* a race. A team works best when it works together and its members stay committed to one another. Is that understood?"

"Yes, Coach."

"Blake, front and center."

Blake stepped forward and approached Coach Tomlin.

"It's admirable that you wanted to stand up for your friend, but it's troubling you were going to take down a bully with your fists. That's not the way you should resolve it, at least not here; there are other ways to deal with bullies. I want you to figure that out, because if I catch you in a school fight, I guarantee you will not only be suspended but you will be off this team as well. I can't have four players off the team, so get your shit together and keep your temper under control. Is that clear?" the coach asked.

"Yes, sir," Blake answered.

"All right, that's enough for today. Everyone, have a great weekend. Go shower up, and no monkey business in the showers. If there's any fighting or any more horse shit going on, there will be hell to pay on Monday. Track team, fall out!"

Blake watched the team walk off the track field. Quinn sidled up to him.

"Dude, were you channeling your inner *Teen Wolf* back there?" Quinn asked.

"Maybe."

"That was awesome!"

"Well, it worked on the show, so I figured it was worth a try."

"I can't believe he did that," Blake said, flipping through the pages of the latest Spider-man comic Quinn had just gotten.

"I know," Quinn said, "he's such a jerk."

The boys relaxed on Quinn's queen-sized bed. That night, the central air conditioning struggled to keep the house cool.

"I just don't understand why he thinks it's okay to pick on other people. Don't we see enough of this on TV, and haven't we learned it's not okay?" Blake asked.

Quinn shrugged. "The world seems to be built on conflict. Everyone fights."

Blake chuckled. "If only you knew." *You have no idea how much people fight. Your parents are angels compared to the demons I live with.*

"Well, at least we don't fight like that," Blake said.

"Like what?" Quinn asked.

"Oh, right," Blake answered. "Well, like my parents, for starters. And you and I don't fight or treat each other like crap, like Darien does everyone else."

"Naw," Quinn said, "we're good. I like to think we're above that kind of stuff...that we know it's better to help each other and help others instead of beating each other up and tearing one another down."

A knock sounded at the open door. Blake looked up to see Mr. McAlester—or Daddio—standing there.

"You boys about ready to crash?" he asked. "We have an early morning ahead of us."

"Yep, we will in just a few minutes," Quinn said. "Good night, Daddio."

"Good night, guys," Daddio said.

"Good night, Mr. Mac," Blake said, using the affectionate nickname he had given Daddio.

Quinn's father left the room, and the boys decided to get ready for bed.

"I'm going to brush my teeth," Quinn said, rolling off his bed.

"I will, too," Blake said, following Quinn into the bathroom.

Together they stood at the sink, staring aimlessly at each other and the tooth-brushes in their hands as they brushed their teeth.

Quinn stepped to the toilet, and with his back to Blake, began to pee. The long-standing friendship the boys shared had tore down most of the barriers between them, and there wasn't much the boys didn't share or know about one another.

Blake spat toothpaste foam into the sink and grabbed Quinn's mouthwash. He swigged some and swished it around his mouth. Several seconds later, he spat that out too. When Quinn finished using the toilet, it was Blake's turn.

The boys headed back into Quinn's room, and Blake crawled onto the right side of the bed. Quinn shut the door and turned the air conditioning up, then approached his side of the bed. The boys had been sharing a bed during sleepovers since they'd been kids, and they didn't see a reason to stop sharing a bed just because they had gotten older or because of what Darien would think if he ever found out.

Blake picked up his comic book and idly stared at the colorful pages. "I'm really glad your dads let me come with you this weekend."

"Me too," Quinn said, pulling off his shirt and jumping into bed. He wore only his boxers. "I'm glad your parents let you come."

"Meh," Blake said, sitting up and pulling off his T-shirt. "My parents don't care. You know that."

"I know," Quinn said, "I just keep hoping—"

"Don't bother," Blake said, lying down. "I stopped hoping a long time ago. It is what it is, and I only have to deal with it for two more years."

"Well, we're gonna have a good time this weekend," Quinn said, "so I hope we can forget all the bad shit that's going on. Not that there's a lot of bad shit, but you know."

"Yeah, I hear ya," Blake said. "I'm sorry, I'm just sort of bummed today. I'll be in a better mood tomorrow. We'll have an awesome time, I promise."

"Great," Quinn said, "You can keep reading, but I'm going to bed. I'm wiped."

"Me too. Let's kill the lights."

They each turned off the lamp on the nightstand next to their side of the bed and then rolled over and fell asleep.

Chapter 4
Family Camping Trip

Quinn

"We're here," Daddio announced, waking the occupants of the car.

Quinn opened his eyes and blinked in the bright daylight. When they'd left Portsmouth at six thirty, the sun had barely risen, but now at nine thirty it shone brightly through the trees.

"Thank goodness," Blake said.

"What do you mean, 'Thank goodness'?" Dad asked, smiling as he shot Blake a quick glance. "You slept the entire way. We're the ones who stayed awake to make sure you got here safely."

"Yeah, yeah," Blake said, smiling in the back seat. Quinn yawned and stretched his hands over the front seat, gently massaging the trapezius muscles of his dad.

"Thanks for making sure we got here safe, dads. It's gonna be an awesome weekend."

"I can't believe I slept the whole way," Blake said.

"We can't either," Daddio said, chuckling.

Quinn said, "I didn't think we were that tired, but I guess yesterday's run through New Castle really wiped us out."

"I agree with you," Blake said. "Did we hit any traffic?"

"Not really," Daddio said. "We left early enough that all the Massachusetts folk heading into Maine this morning weren't even out of bed yet."

"Great," Quinn said. "I'm glad that was so easy."

Fifteen minutes later, Daddio checked them into Woods Lake Campground. Then, they drove the vehicle to the campsite, and when they had parked, they climbed out to stretch their legs. Daddio went to the back of the SUV and opened the tailgate while Dad walked around and explored the camping area.

"Well, if our fireplace is right there, then I guess maybe we should put our two tents over there. What do you guys think?" Dad asked, pointing as he spoke.

"Sounds good to me."

"Me too," Blake added, agreeing with his best friend.

"Okay then, let's set up our tents," Dad said.

Quinn nodded and grabbed his red tent from the back of the vehicle. Then, he and Blake walked over to an area and checked for small rocks and tree roots.

"The ground is dry here, so this should be a good spot. What do you think?" Blake asked.

"Works for me," Quinn agreed.

Quinn started unpacking the tent, and Blake helped. Alongside them, Dad and Daddio unpacked and set up their tent.

"Are you sure you don't want us to set up the big family tent?" Dad asked, teasing his son.

"No thanks, Dad," Quinn said. "I'm sure you guys would love some privacy." Blake chuckled.

"Aw," Daddio said. "You don't want to have family time with us anymore?"

Quinn rolled his eyes and smiled. "You know what I mean. So, uh, Dad, you should move your tent over about ten feet."

Dad smiled and said, "sounds good to me." Then he winked at the boys.

"Oh man," Blake said.

"Tell me about it," Quinn added. "Maybe we should go ten feet in the other direction," he said, winking at his best friend.

"Hey, it won't hurt. The woods are pretty quiet at night, if you know what I mean."

The dads and the boys moved their tents farther apart. Once Quinn and Blake had staked their tent in the ground, they inserted the support poles and raised the tent into position. When the boys finished, Quinn grabbed the air mattress and Blake grabbed the air pump. They took turns inflating it, and when they were done, Daddio handed them their air mattress.

"Since you boys did such a great job with yours, I'm sure you wouldn't mind blowing ours up."

Quinn and Blake smiled, and Quinn said, "No, of course not."

As the boys worked, Dad and Daddio grabbed the faded red picnic table from the far end of the site and moved it closer to the fireplace. Now their tents were on each side of the clearing, and the fireplace and picnic table were in the middle. After setting up a rain shelter near the dads' tent, Dad strung a rope from one tree to the other for the clothesline while Daddio grabbed some of the coolers and set them on the picnic table.

"Are you guys hungry now?" Daddio asked. "We got up early and—"

"Yes, we're teenagers, we're always hungry," Quinn said.

Blake smiled and added, "What he said."

"Well, I don't have anything ready to cook, but we have some protein bars and snack foods. So dig in." He pulled a ziplock bag full of snacks from one of the food bags and set it on the picnic table. He checked his watch. "It's a bit too early for the meats and cheeses, so I think we should—"

"Wait," Quinn said, "did you really make meats and cheeses? Like a charcuterie for a cutting board with fancy meats and cheeses?"

His dad offered a guilty smile. "Maybe."

"You're ridiculous, Daddio," Quinn said.

"Hey," he said, "just because we're camping doesn't mean it can't be a fabulous time. Right, hon?"

"That's right," Dad called from the other side of the tent, his back to them.

"What are you doing?" Quinn asked.

"Watering this pine tree! Mind your own business."

"Oh, okay."

After they ate some snacks, the boys unloaded their sleeping and duffle bags from the car and set everything inside their tent. It was spacious, so they had plenty of room to spread out comfortably.

"Actually," Daddio said, looking at his watch again, "it's late enough in the morning that if we used the gas grill, we could have some burgers and dogs and then head off to the beach for the afternoon. What do you think?"

"Sounds great," Blake said.

"That's awesome, let's do it," Quinn said.

Dad nodded. Together, the dads lugged the grilling equipment from the back of the vehicle and set it up on the other side of the picnic table. Quinn and Blake shifted some of the coolers around so there would be more room and they would have a place to eat. Fifteen minutes later, pre-made hamburger patties and hot dogs were sizzling on the grill while Dad buttered some buns and placed them on the outer edges of the grill, so they would brown.

"What do you guys want to drink?" Quinn asked, knowing the answer.

"I'm going to have some root beer," Daddio said.

"Me too," Dad said.

"Blake?" Quinn asked.

"Uh, pick a soda for me."

Quinn smiled with gratitude as he pulled four root beers from the cooler. He knew his dads discreetly sacrificed alcoholic drinks because they understood Blake's father drank at any point in the day and they didn't want to cause his best friend any undue stress or worry. A few minutes later, the guys enjoyed their first camping meal together.

"Oh no, I forgot the chips," Daddio said through a mouthful of hamburger.

"No, you didn't," Quinn said. "I think they're in a bag over here."

"Oh, thank heavens! I can't have a burger without chips," Dad said.

Quinn rummaged through some bags near him and pulled out the bag of salt and pepper potato chips. "Camping trip disaster averted," he said, winking at his father.

"Thank heavens!" Daddio echoed, winking at his son.

"By the way, Dad, where's your cell phone?" Quinn asked, looking at his father.

Dad smiled and pulled it out of his pocket. "Here you go. Just keep it nearby and in a safe place so that if we need it, I'm not panicking for it."

"No problem," Quinn said. "I'll make sure it's inside the lock box in the vehicle."

"Do I have to turn in my phone?" Daddio asked.

"That depends," Quinn said. "Will your office be texting you or emailing you, and will you be checking it throughout the weekend?"

"No, of course not."

"Then you're safe," Quinn responded.

"Yay," Daddio said, winking at his husband.

"But I don't expect you to be on it, just like Blake and I are putting our phones away as well."

"We are?" Blake asked, looking up through a mouthful of hot dog. "I didn't know that."

Quinn smiled. "New rules, I guess."

Blake shrugged. "I don't have cell service up here, so I'll keep my phone on me."

"Fine."

"Oh," Daddio said, raising his phone. "I don't have cell service up here, either. I guess the office couldn't reach me even if they wanted to."

"Good," Quinn said.

"I'm a little surprised there's no service," Dad said. "You'd think that would be important around a campground."

"Especially since we're not exactly close to civilization up here. Still, it's beautiful," Daddio said.

"Like you."

"Aw, you're too sweet."

"Thank you."

"Do you guys need some special couple time in your tent?" Quinn asked.

Blake laughed and spit a mouthful of root beer across the forest floor, narrowly missing Quinn.

"It can wait," Dad said.

"But not too long," Daddio chimed in.

"Whatever," Quinn said, smiling.

Quinn pulled off his shirt, rolled it into a ball, and tossed it onto the beach towel he had laid out. Blake, sitting next to him, applied sunscreen to his chest. Quinn reached for his bottle of sunscreen and did the same.

"I can't believe how beautiful it is up here," Blake commented. "And there's like, no one around, either."

"It's early," Dad said. "I bet other campers will make their way to the beach over the next two hours."

"Sounds like a good time for a nap then," his husband replied, winking the obviousness of his double entendre into the universe.

Quinn and Blake stared at each other with mild embarrassment and shook their heads. When Blake finished applying his sunscreen, he handed the bottle to Quinn, who applied it to his back. They switched off, and so did the dads. Finishing up, they all laid out on their beach towels and relaxed as they soaked in the late summer sun.

Sometime later, Quinn propped himself up on his elbows so he could watch the water in front of him. A few children played in the pond with their parents. On the other side, some other teenagers kept to themselves, but occasionally laughed about the conversation he couldn't hear. An elderly couple was walking on the small beach together, each one holding sandals in their hand as they held each other's hand.

"Wow," Daddio commented, pointing to the sky. "The clouds around here are really weird. Look at all the crazy shapes and things you can see in them."

"That must be because of the mountains," Dad said.

"Interesting."

"That one looks like a dagger or a submarine," Quinn said, pointing at a cloud to the left.

Blake propped himself up and shielded his eyes from the sun. "It does. And that one looks like a dog or a cat. More like a dog, I think."

"How about that one over there, Blake? What do you think that looks like?" Dad asked.

"Um…" Blake started, unsure of what he was looking at.

"I don't even know what that looks like," Quinn chimed in.

"Neither did I. I was just curious to know if you did."

They laughed together and laid back down. Daddio picked up his Kindle and started reading, holding it up to shield his eyes from the sun.

"I thought we were here to relax?" Dad asked, glancing at his husband.

"We are," Daddio said. "Reading fiction is relaxing."

"Yes, but it's an electronic device."

"It's an allowed electronic device," Daddio said, smiling. "Or has the judge and jury not weighed in on that yet?" he asked, looking at Quinn and Blake.

"Don't worry, Mr. Mac," Blake said, smiling, "if it becomes a problem, your Kindle isn't waterproof."

Daddio smiled. "You wouldn't dare!"

Quinn turned his voice into a creepy old man's voice and said, "Do what must be done. Show no mercy."

Dad burst out laughing. "*Now* he quotes Star Wars."

"Hey," Quinn said, "when it works, it works." Quinn smiled, knowing it would be a great couple of days with his family and best friend. He took a deep breath inside and enjoyed the warm feeling of the sun caressing his face and torso.

Several hours later, after swimming in the pond and playing an impromptu game of water volleyball, Quinn's dads left the beach to take a nap back at their campsite. Quinn and Blake decided to stay behind and give the dads some privacy.

"We should go exploring later," Quinn said, applying more sunscreen to his body.

"Definitely," Blake agreed. "What do you want to explore?"

"I saw some hiking trails on the campground map. Other than that, there isn't a whole lot, but at least we have GPS in our cell phones."

"Our cell phones aren't working."

"Oh. Right. Well, like I said, we can explore those trails at some point or just walk around the campground. We're not exactly on a treasure hunt here. It's not like we're gonna find some big mystery."

"Okay, well, maybe later tonight or tomorrow morning we can go exploring."

"How about tomorrow morning?" Quinn asked. "I think my dads would really enjoy our company tonight. I think they have a special campfire thing planned with s'mores and other fun stuff."

"That sounds really exciting. Thanks again for letting me come with you," Blake said.

"Of course," Quinn answered. "Why wouldn't you be here?" he asked, feeling surprised.

"Well, it's just that…I don't know…my parents aren't always—"

"Never mind them," Quinn interrupted. "Our lives are our lives, and I'm glad you're in mine."

Quinn rubbed the after-sun aloe lotion in his hands and rubbed it on Blake's back. Although they hadn't burned, they'd spent a lot of time in the sun, and their dry skin needed aloe. Quinn finished, handed the bottle to Blake, and turned around. Blake spread the lotion on Quinn's back. The boys had just washed up at the campground's shower cabin and were getting ready to head back to their campsite and tent for the night.

"I'm stuffed," Quinn said, holding his distended stomach.

"Yeah, totally shouldn't have had those last couple of s'mores. Daddio did a great job with the grilled chicken, too."

Quinn nodded. Several days ago, his dad had marinated chicken breasts that he grilled for dinner.

"All set," Blake said, rubbing the excess lotion on his chest. "I hate sleeping with this stuff on me. My skin feels clammy and gross, especially in this wicked humidity."

"Yeah, but at least your skin will feel better tomorrow," Quinn said, wiping the extra lotion on his hands over his chest and arms.

"Almost done?" Blake asked, grabbing his shower tote.

"Yup," Quinn answered. He finished and grabbed his towel and toiletry bag. "Let's go."

Back at the tent, Quinn settled in first and lay on top of his open sleeping bag wearing only plaid boxer shorts. He rested his hands behind his head and watched the heat lightning flash above them through the screened air vents in the tent. The evening air had not cooled off, a surprising happenstance given how far north they were on Labor Day weekend.

Blake climbed onto his sleeping bag, making the shared air mattress under Quinn bounce as he settled down. In the distance, a light rumble of thunder echoed through the campground.

"I think I want to come out to my dads soon," Quinn said softly.

Blake chuckled. "It's about time."

"I know, I know. They're gay, and obviously they won't care, but I just think it's still a big deal. I mean, I get teased at school for being gay and—"

"No, you get teased for not being out. That and you're too nice, and the bullies know they can pick on you."

A bright flash of lightning made Quinn blink. "Darien picks on you, too, buddy."

"Yeah, but not in the same way he picks on you." A clap of thunder, much closer, rumbled through the night air. The wind picked up as well and shook the tent.

"You know your dads must have a clue, right?"

"What do you mean?" Quinn asked, turning to look at his friend.

"You don't date girls. You don't talk about girls. And let's face it, you're one snappy dresser."

"Yeah, but that could just be because they trained me—"

"Nope, it's not. It's not because you have gay dads." More lightning flashed, followed by a serious thunderclap. "Your family is going to love and accept you no matter what, because that's who they are. You're lucky that way," Blake said, becoming somber as he stared at a piece of lint on the air mattress between them.

Quinn's brow furled, and he looked at his friend. "Why, are *you* gonna come out or something? Shouldn't you tell *me* first?"

"No," Blake said, shaking his head a little. "I just...my parents don't care about me. I mean, my older sister has been out of the house for what, two years now? My parents never mention her, and they treat me like shit. They don't care, Quinn."

Quinn contemplated his response as a gust of wind rattled the tent.

"Boys!" Dad called out. "Let's get in the car before it rains. Close up your tent!"

"Okay," Quinn answered back, sitting up. "We'll get back to this," he said, gently squeezing Blake's shoulder.

"Yup," Blake said. "Let's avoid certain death for now, though, right?"

Quinn smiled and stood up. He and Blake grabbed flashlights and zipped up all the air vents and then stepped out into the night air.

"Should we get dressed?" Blake asked, looking down at his boxer shorts.

"We're only going to the car...unless you really want to." A wild flash of lightning and a blast of wind surged through the air. A moment later, thunder cracked overhead.

"Hell no," Blake said, zipping up the doorway of the tent. They stepped into their flip-flops and then jogged across the campsite to the car, where the dads were waiting for them in a similar state of undress. Drops of water fell and began pelting them. As the four car doors slammed shut, a double flash of lightning announced the oncoming downpour as wind and thunder shook up the skies.

"That was good timing," Quinn said. A thick, jagged arc of lightning split the sky in half as earsplitting thunder tumbled across the campsite.

"You're not kidding," Blake said. "I thought it was only supposed to be heat lightning, but I guess I—"

"Whoa!" All four guys shouted as several bright flashes illuminated the forest in front of them. The ensuing crack-boom vibrated the plastic interior of the car and all of the campground's light-sensitive lamps went dark, the bright lightning having tricked the sensors into thinking it was daylight.

"That had to hit something," Daddio said. "At least, it sounded like it hit something."

The rain intensified, and Quinn couldn't see more than a few feet in front of him. They watched the freak storm in silence, making small talk. When they could see through the torrential rain, the trees appeared bent like bows as they struggled to retain their rooting in the ground and stand against the driving wind and rain. At three different points, the guys heard several deep thudding sounds that made the SUV shudder under them.

Then, twenty minutes later, just as quickly as it had arrived, the storm disappeared. "Well, at least one good thing came out of this," Daddio announced after he opened his door. "Sleeping tonight just got a lot easier."

Quinn stepped into the night and felt the cool, dry air around him. The storm had broken through the thick soup of humidity and offered relief until the next day. Together, they walked back to their tents.

"Sleep well, boys," Dad said. "If we get another storm, back to the car." He jerked his thumb back toward the SUV.

"Good night," Quinn and Blake said together.

Since the lights were still out, they and other campers used flashlights to return to their tents. When the boys finished re-opening their tent, they climbed into their sleeping bags for the night.

Chapter 5

The Day Everything Changed

Blake

B lake opened his eyes and shut them quickly. *Damn, that's bright.*

Red-tinted sunlight that filtered through the tent's red nylon sides filled the inside of the tent. He shivered at the cool morning air on his exposed chest and pulled his sleeping bag up to his neck. He glanced over at Quinn, who slept on his side, facing him. Blake smirked when he saw a bit of drool leaking from his buddy's mouth.

He reached over and gently pressed his index finger against the tip of Quinn's nose.

Quinn cracked open an eye and met his gaze. "Morning," he said, rolling on to his back, raising his arms above his head, and stretching his legs in his sleeping bag.

"Hi," Blake answered, still sleepy. The air mattress gently shifted as Blake sat up and stretched his arms up over his head. "I'm ready to get up and go exploring or something."

Quinn groaned. "No, it's too early. What's wrong with you? I need five more minutes, okay?"

"Nope!" Blake reached over and patted his hands on Quinn's chest. "Time to get up!"

Quinn laughed and slapped Blake's hands away. "Fine, fine, whatever."

The boys pulled on some gym shorts and stepped out of the tent, sliding their feet into their flip-flops. Blake looked around the campsite. A few other colorful tents dotted the tree line, and two families with younger children were already cooking breakfast several sites over. Otherwise, it was quiet.

"Whoa," Blake said, his eyes landing on a pile of tall pine trees that had been knocked over during the storm. "How come we didn't hear those fall?"

Quinn stared at the trees and rubbed his eyes again. "I thought I felt the car shake a couple of times. That must have been why."

"Right, I remember the shaking."

"Good thing there were no tents under there. Those people would have been seriously hurt, or worse. Even the SUV wouldn't have protected us from falling trees."

Blake looked over to the other tent. "Your dads aren't up yet."

"Weird, they're usually early birds."

"Maybe they're taking advantage of the quiet. Maybe we should, too, while no one's really up yet. Wanna go shower?"

"Sure," Quinn said.

After grabbing their towels and toiletry bags, the boys zipped up the tent and ambled over to the shower facilities. When they arrived at the shower cabin, the lights wouldn't work and the water pressure was non-existent.

"Power must be out," Blake said. "Must be a ton of trees down or something."

"Most likely. Um, I'm gonna go jump in the pond and rinse off the sleepiness."

"Great idea."

The boys splashed around in their boxer shorts for a while in the cool waters of Quimby pond. After, they made their way back to their campsite and got dressed for the morning. When they finished putting on shorts and tank tops, Quinn poked his head out and checked on his dads. "They're still not up."

"Then let's go exploring. Maybe they'll be up in an hour or whatever."

"Sounds good." Blake reached for a clean pair of socks and his sneakers.

Moments later, the boys trekked to the marked trailhead at the edge of camp that offered several routes through the forest and around the pond.

"Which way do you want to go?" Quinn asked.

Blake spun his arm through the air and pointed to one of the trails that led away from the campsite and the pond. "That way," he said, pointing to the trail. On the first tree, an old, faded sign asked hikers to *Please stay on trails.*

"I wish I had some coffee," Quinn complained. Then he let loose a big yawn and started walking down the trail.

"You could have made some," Blake responded.

"My dads have the car keys."

"Oh, right. Why are you so tired?"

"I dunno. Too much time in the sun yesterday?"

"Could be."

Nature chirped and buzzed around them as various birds and insects set about their very busy day of foraging and whatever else the wild things of the woods do. Several chipmunks squeaked their displeasure and scampered into the underbrush as the boys' heavy and energetic footsteps alerted anything within earshot that two teenage humans were approaching.

The trails were still muddy from the storm's rainfall, and the boys laughed and zigzagged around large puddles and tried not to lose their balance on slippery tree roots. Occasionally they diverted from the trail because the leafy ground was drier and less menacing than the flattened and waterlogged trail they followed.

Ten minutes later, Quinn stopped and stared at something to his right. "Whoa, check that out," he said, pointing to a line of pine trees that had been knocked over by the storm winds.

Blake looked over and became interested in the fallen trees. "Let's follow them and see where it goes," Blake said. "There might be a pot of gold at the end of the tree line."

"Eh," Quinn said, looking around.

"We're not going to get lost," Blake said, anticipating his best buddy's objections. "All we have to do is follow the broken trees back, see? It cuts right across the trail we're on."

"Okay," Quinn said, nodding. "Let's do it."

Blake led the way as the boys hopped over shattered tree trunks and wondered at the massive root systems of uprooted trees the storm winds had blown over like toothpicks.

"There had to be a mini-tornado-micro-burst-thing last night," Quinn said. "That's the only thing that explains this. There's no way a bunch of trees would fall like dominos in the woods."

"Sure as hell was windy enough for one. Like you said earlier, I'm glad this didn't come through the campground. Still, this is too close for comfort."

Several minutes later, they made it to the end of the fallen trees and stopped. "Well, this is less exciting than I thought it would be," Blake said. They looked around for a moment at the various trees, ferns, and other foliage that grew around them. A hawk or an eagle—Blake wasn't sure which—screeched above them in the sky.

"Or is it?" Quinn said, pointing at something on their left. "What the heck is that big rock thing?"

Blake look at Quinn's arm and followed the pointed finger toward a strange-looking, geometrically shaped rock in the ground. Near it, several bushes had been uprooted. "Whatever it is, the storm winds exposed it. Let's check it out."

"Yeah, it looks cool."

The boys made their way over to the rock.

As they approached, Blake saw it was not a rock or a boulder but a lichen- and moss-covered concrete bunker-looking box sunken into the earth. On the right side, two angular sides or fins protruded out, inviting a closer inspection. They made their way around to the fins and discovered they were supporting walls that sheltered a medium-sized stairwell that descended into the darkness of a tunnel. A weathered metal sign hung above the entrance, its message clear: *Keep Out.*

"That's not meant for us," Blake said, smiling wickedly. "Right?"

"Of course not," Quinn answered, looking at his friend with mock indignation. "I'm sure whoever put that sign up did *not* intend it for two teenagers on an exploratory mission to discover the deep, dark secrets of Rangeley, Maine."

"Exactly what I was thinking."

Blake hunched as he descended the bunker's worn stairs carefully and then stood up in the entrance. *I'm glad this was built for tall people.*

"You didn't happen to bring a flashlight, did you?" Quinn asked as he made his way down the stairs. "We won't be able to go very far."

"I have my phone's flashlight."

"You brought your cell phone? Even though it has no signal?"

"Force of habit." He shrugged.

"Good point."

Blake pulled his phone out of his pocket, tapped on flashlight mode, and then led the way into the tunnel. It descended slightly as they made their way inside. He felt the cool dampness of the tunnel walls around him on his skin. Occasionally, roots poked through cracks in the concrete, and dripping water seeped through at other points. The air smelled of damp earth and plant matter, but it didn't seem moldy or musty.

About fifty feet in, the darkness engulfed them, and Quinn put his hand on Blake's shoulder.

"Train tracks?" Quinn asked, pointing at the ground ahead of them.

"Yup," Blake said, shining his light downward. A set of miniature railroad tracks abruptly ended in front of them as if they had been ripped out from that point to the entrance of the cave. However, the tracks continued as they made their way deeper into the tunnel.

"Looks like a mining tunnel of some kind, like in Indiana Jones," Quinn quipped.

"If there are monster snakes, spiders, or flame-throwing savages in here, I'm out."

"We're in Maine, Blake. None of those things exist in Maine. It probably just dead-ends anyway."

"You never know," Blake said, carefully stepping on the old wooden ties that connected the rusting rails together.

After a few more steps, Quinn squeezed Blake's arm. He stopped moving and looked over his shoulder, even though he couldn't see his friend's face.

"What?" Blake asked.

"Sssh. What's that noise?"

"You're being an ass."

"No, I'm serious. It's like a humming sound."

Blake exhaled and concentrated on the sounds within the tunnel. Quinn was right; a strange humming resonated in the tunnel around them.

"It sounds mechanical."

"Or electrical," Quinn added. "It's like, thrumming or something. Let's keep going."

"Okay." Blake continued walking forward, and Quinn kept his hand on his shoulder. The closer they got to whatever was on the other side of the tunnel, the louder the sound became.

"It's actually pulsing very slowly," Quinn whispered.

"Yeah," Blake said, noting the rise and fall of the oscillating energy noise.

"How deep do you think we are?" Quinn asked.

"I have no idea." They stopped and turned around to look behind them. The entrance to the tunnel was a small dot far in the distance above them.

"We're a heck of a lot farther in than I thought," Quinn said.

"I don't think we have far to go," Blake said. "I see blue light ahead of us."

"Oh, you're right! That's so cool…I mean weird, what's a blue light doing underground?"

Blake chuckled. "Let's go find out." The boys pressed on and made their way to the end of the tunnel where their path was blocked by a large, rusting metal door. In the space between the door and the threshold, blue light glowed brightly when the sound became louder and dimmed when the sound became softer.

"Do you think it's locked?" Quinn whispered, shuffling up to the door.

"How the hell do I know?" Blake whispered back.

"Wait, there's no lock," Quinn said, pointing at the pull-style door handle. "Why is there no lock?"

"We're in the middle of nowhere Maine, that's why."

Quinn nodded and looked at Blake in the dim light. "Should we?"

"We didn't come all this way not to," Blake said, reaching for the handle.

"Wait, turn off your flashlight. If there's someone in there, I don't want them to see us right away."

"Good point." Blake turned off the flashlight app and put his phone into the pocket of his shorts. "Well, here goes nothing." He reached out, grabbed the door knob, and pulled.

Nothing.

He pulled a little harder.

Still nothing.

"It won't open," he whispered.

"Let's try together," Quinn suggested.

"Okay."

They both wrapped their hand around the knob.

Quinn counted off for them. "One, two, three…" They pulled together, and the door made a strange creaking sound that echoed in the tunnel, but it didn't open.

"I think it budged a little. Maybe it's just rusted shut," Quinn whispered. "Let's try again and really pull. Just wait for the noise to get loud."

"Okay."

They both grabbed the knob again, and as the humming became loud again, Quinn counted off. "One, two, three…"

The door yielded to their combined strength and jerked open in their hands, causing them to stumble back as a powerful light source bathed them in brilliant hues of blue. Then, the light dimmed as the oscillating humming sound faded. Blake looked at Quinn, who looked at him with wide eyes that shifted between the open door and Blake's eyes.

Blake listened as well.

Nothing.

There was no sound other than the weird humming with the blue lights. Quinn jerked his head to the open door, and Blake nodded.

Blake pulled the door open, and the two boys stepped through it, the old door closer hissing as it slowly pulled the door shut behind them. He glanced at the door frame one last time to make sure there were no locks on it. The last thing he wanted was to be trapped underground in someone's weird science experiment.

"Wow, it looks a lot like the X-Men's Cerebro in here," Quinn said, pointing to the ceiling of whatever they were in.

Blake followed his buddy's finger up to the neatly arranged metallic-looking silver-and-blue hexagonal plates around them. His eyes adjusted to the darkness and the oscillating pattern of the blue light.

"Dude, this has to be alien. Did we just discover an alien spaceship?" Quinn asked excitedly.

"With a concrete bunker and old mining tracks attached to it? Unlikely."

"But what if those were added after it crashed?" Quinn said, becoming more daring and stepping into the center of the thing Blake decided was a cool-looking, futuristic geometric dome.

"Uh-huh," Blake said. His sneaker splashed in a small puddle. Glancing down, he noticed the rocky ground was wet. He returned his gaze to the domed chamber around him. The interior was about thirty feet in diameter and contained only two doors: the one they came through and the one on the opposite side. The topmost point of the dome above them had to be seventy-five feet up. In the center of the dome's ceiling, a glowing blue-white ring on a conical silver thing with three upside-down antenna arrays sent pulses of blue-white light outward across the top of the dome through eight translucent tubes placed between the hexagonal plates that lined the chamber's walls. The eight tubes demarcated the eight sides of the octagonal chamber and traveled down the walls into the rock floor where they directed the energy-light they carried toward a six-foot-in-diameter ring of swirling, spinning blue-white energy set in the center of the floor. Inside the circle of the light, a metal disc covered the rock floor. Blake assumed the energy traveled farther into the ground, but he didn't understand how.

"Look, a hatch," Quinn said, pointing toward an open hatch in the floor to one side of the dome.

"Good thing we didn't miss that and fall through it," Blake commented.

Quinn walked to the open hatch and squatted, straining to see its secrets. "There's more light down here, and a ladder." He looked up at Blake, who nodded.

"Go ahead, it's not like anyone's here."

Quinn climbed through the hatch and made his way down the metal ladder. Blake squatted near the top and waited.

"There's a lot more of that blue light stuff, and I can see where it goes through the floor. There's nothing down here but a bunch of big boxes."

What the heck kind of place is this? Weird lights, strange sounds, a man-made—or alien—underground dome thing, and now a room full of big boxes?

"I think they're batteries," Quinn called up from the floor below. "They look like really big car batteries, and they go on and on. The room down here is way bigger than the cave you're standing in. There's also this big silver thing under the middle of the cave that has tons of wires going out from it, but each box has only two wires going to the only two terminals I can see on them. They all have lots of green lights, too."

"Cool," Blake said. He stood up and turned around, more curious about the place than ever. *So now we have batteries under the floor...*

Quinn climbed back up the ladder and shut the hatch behind him.

"I don't think those are fancy lights," Blake said, tucking his hands into the pockets of his shorts.

"What do you mean?"

"I mean, it's electricity..." Blake raised his arm and waved it through the air. He stopped and stared at his arm hair; it was not standing on end. "No, it's not electricity, but it's some kind of energy. This entire room is gathering energy from somewhere and converting it for storage beneath us."

"Wicked," Quinn said, taking in Blake's hypothesis.

"That means there must be something above the ground collecting the energy, right?"

"That makes sense. So, if it's collecting energy from above ground, it's converting it in here and storing it below us. But why is *this* energy moving so slow? We can't see electricity moving except in lightning, and that's friggin' fast."

"I didn't say I figured it all out, buddy," Blake answered, chuckling.

"What are they storing it for?" Quinn asked. "Do you think this is what solar panel energy looks like?"

Blake slouched his shoulders and rolled his eyes at Quinn. "Really?"

"I'm kidding. But what other kind of energy gets collected above ground? This isn't hydroelectric, and there's no dam near here. At least, I don't think there is, because we should hear running water and turbines."

Blake shrugged.

Quinn walked to the closest energy tube and stared at the pulsing blue-white light traveling through it. "These are conduits, then. I wonder what all the metal plates are for?" He turned around and looked at the hexagonal plates that lined the chamber.

"What do the metal plates do in Cerebro?" Blake asked.

"Well, amplify and focus, I guess."

"Uh-huh."

"You think this thing works like made-up comic book technology?" Quinn ran to the center of the room and jumped over the ring of light, landing on the metal disk in the center.

Blake nodded. "If this is a conversion chamber, then yeah. I think it's why the energy moves slowly through those tubes. I just don't know what it's amplifying or focusing." He followed Quinn onto the metal disc thing.

Above them, the loud clang of a mechanical switch flipping echoed in the chamber. Quinn gasped with fright and Blake nearly jumped out of his skin. The quick whine of a heavy motor activating beneath them pulled Blake's attention to the metal disk they stood on.

"What the hell?" Quinn said, his index finger pointing up at the ceiling.

Blake ignored the rumbling floor and looked up. "Holy shit!"

The blue-white ring of energy-light was spinning quickly, releasing a shimmering cascade of energy into the chamber. The conical thing with the three antennas moved down toward them, and the pulsing energy sound increased its cadence and speed at the same time.

"Look at the walls," Quinn said. Blake looked over and saw the downward-flowing streams of energy-light in the eight tubes had reversed. They rapidly flowed upward to the pulsing ring at the top of the dome.

"We need to get out of here," Quinn said, turning to run back to the door they entered from.

Blake looked down and couldn't see the chamber floor around the disk. *This metal floor thing elevated itself!*

"No wait, don't!" Blake yelled. He grabbed at Quinn's arm and pulled him back from the edge of the disk—now realized as a platform. "We're, like, ten feet off the ground!"

"What?" Quinn exclaimed, looking around them.

Suddenly, the sound of an energy surge rapidly charging and discharging filled the chamber. Quinn spun around and grabbed Blake's arms. Without thought, Blake grabbed Quinn's arms, and the two boys looked into each other's widened eyes, fearing the worst.

"I love you, buddy, but I think we're fu—"

The blue and white energy swirls above them exploded downward with a blinding flash and a deafening blast. Too stunned to move, Blake looked down and watched the metal disk glow yellow as it reacted with the energy swirling around them.

The disk beneath them shook as a second, much louder rapid energy blast rose from the ground, moved to the ceiling, and then stopped.

The boys looked up and winced.

A cascade of energy rocketed downward and surged through their bodies, energizing them. The breath in Blake's throat became stuck, as he could not inhale or exhale in the moment. Blake felt all the muscles in his body constrict, especially the ones gripping Quinn's arms. Quinn's fingers tightened on his arms as well. Blake felt the hair on his head, arms, and legs stand on end as the powerful rush of strange energy surged through his body.

Quinn's mouth fell open and his facial expression conveyed terror.

Blake found the strength to shift his eyes downward to look at Quinn and watched as blue sparks and arcs of energy jumped between the upper and lower teeth of Quinn's open mouth, occasionally arcing on his tongue as well. He saw his best friend's eyes glow an extremely bright shade of blue as they met Blake's gaze. For Blake, everything around him turned bright orange. The roar of energy and raw power in the room was deafening, but just as mysteriously as it started, it stopped.

The disk-platform they stood on lowered and retracted into the floor. Soon, the boys were back on ground level, shaking as they held one another in fright.

"I…I think we're alive," Blake said.

Quinn turned and fell to his knees, dry-heaving.

Above them, the same clang of a mechanical switch flipping echoed in the chamber. Blake looked up. The conical antenna array had retracted up as well, and the chamber seemed to have reset itself. This time, no energy moved in the tubes.

"We need to get out of here," Blake said, pulling Quinn up. They stumbled together as waves of dizziness and vertigo screwed with their balance. Quinn kept dry-heaving, a sound that challenged Blake's increasing nausea.

"Your eyes," Quinn sputtered, glancing at him, "they're glowing orange."

Blake looked at Quinn and gasped. "Your eyes are glowing blue! Now come on, let's go."

Blake pulled Quinn up once more. They made it to the door, and Blake pushed it open, noting how hot it felt to the touch. Several minutes later, they were out of breath and struggling to make it to the light at the end of the tunnel that twisted and turned in their disoriented vision and sense of balance. Quinn finally stopped dry-heaving, which helped them get out of the tunnel and follow the trees back to the campground trails.

"I...I...," Quinn said, stumbling, unable to utter a sentence. Blake turned and watched his friend collapse to the ground.

"Qu—," Blake tried to say while trying to turn his body around. "Qui—" He fell to his knees, quickly losing all strength in his legs. *Oh no, I'm too young to die. Please, not today.* His vision blurred, and he tried to lie down next to Quinn. *At least...at least they'll know we're...*

Blake collapsed into darkness.

Chapter 6

Web of Lies

Quinn

"We followed the line of fallen trees into the woods," Quinn said, telling a different version of their misadventure to Agent Victor Kraze in their hospital-room-turned-prison cell.

"So, you went off the trails?" Victor asked, his hands folded in his lap.

"Yes," Quinn admitted.

"Fair enough, no judgement here. I probably would have, too. What happened next?"

Quinn looked over at Blake, who shook his head ever so slightly, the kind of nonverbal communication only a close sibling, best friend, or longtime lover would notice and understand.

"Well, we found a whole lot of nothing, to be honest," Quinn lied. "I remember some big boulders, a bunch of weird old sand piles, but we just kept going."

"You wandered into the woods without a compass and working cell phone?" Victor asked, his face expressing surprise.

Blake spoke up. "I had my cell phone with me. I don't know where it is now, but it didn't work anyway."

"The hospital has your cell phone. It should work in here, although cell phones aren't permitted in this wing of the hospital. I'm not sure when you'll get it back, to be honest."

Quinn noted the slight inflection on the last word of Victor's sentence. *I don't care if he's on to us or not. I'm not telling him about the energy thing.*

"What happened next?" Victor asked.

"Well," Quinn said, scrambling to create a believable story Blake could build upon. "We just kept going. I kept looking behind us to make sure we wouldn't lose sight of the fallen trees. It was cool being up in the woods like that, just us in nature."

"Uh-huh," Victor said. "I bet that was special for you two."

Blake laughed.

"Are you boyfriends?" Victor asked.

"What?" Quinn sputtered, trying to sit up. "No, I'm not gay. We're best friends, not boyfriends," he spat out quickly. He relaxed in the bed since the restraints wouldn't let him sit up.

Victor smirked, his face showing his amusement. "Some of that I believe." He sat back in the chair and crossed his legs. "So, two best friends wandered far into the woods to explore what nature has in store for them. Did you see the museum Dr. Madison mentioned?"

Quinn looked at Blake, who shrugged. Victor's eyes bounced between the two boys.

"I don't remember a museum," Blake said, shaking his head.

"Why would there be a museum in the middle of the woods in Maine?" Quinn asked.

Victor smiled. "It's a home, really. It belonged to a scientist named Wilhelm Reich."

"And it's near the campground?"

"Sort of. It's closer to Dodge Pond than Quimby Pond. You'd find it if you hiked due east from the Woods Lake Campground where you were staying."

"Oh."

"Let me piece this back together. You went hiking, discovered the fallen trees, and went exploring on your own in the woods."

"Yup," Blake answered.

"How did you get here?"

"We don't know, Victor," Blake said, glaring at the man. "We were out in the woods and had almost made it back to the trailhead when Quinn complained of nausea and couldn't walk any more. Then I was overcome with nausea, too, and we thought it might be food poisoning from the night before. So, why don't you tell us how we got here?"

"Is that true?" Victor asked, looking at Quinn.

"I guess so, I remember not feeling well and then...I don't know how we got here."

"Okay," Victor said, taking a deep breath. "You were found by a family of hikers. A twelve-year-old girl screamed when she thought she saw two dead bodies lying across the trail. Her mother, who happened to be a nurse, checked your vitals and realized you were alive. After checking you out for any obvious injuries or broken bones, they carried you back—the mom you, Quinn, and the dad you, Blake—to the campground where people struggled to figure out which camping family you belonged to. Medical help was called, and you were transported by ambulance to this medical facility. Blake, your iPhone's emergency medical ID feature told the attending medical staff you were minors and we needed to find your parents. Thank you for making sure that was filled out."

"You're welcome," Blake said.

"The campground organized a small brigade of volunteers that fanned out across the campground with cell phone pictures of your unconscious faces. When someone showed the picture to your dads, they gave verbal consent for basic and emergency treatment until they could get to the hospital."

"Were we treated for anything?" Quinn asked.

"No," Victor answered flatly. "Other than a few bug bites, you have no new scrapes or bruises, which means you didn't fall."

Quinn nodded, playing at remembering something. "You're right, we didn't fall. I remember getting on the ground because I didn't want to fall down," Quinn clarified.

"And I knelt down next to him to help, but when I got dizzy, I laid down."

Victor swirled his tongue around his mouth and took a deep breath. "You were found close to each other, and Blake, you had your hand on Quinn's arm. So that story makes sense to me."

Thank goodness.

"However," Victor continued, "Quinn, your parents did not report any symptoms of food poisoning such as nausea, dizziness, diarrhea, or syncope."

"Or what?" Quinn asked, unfamiliar with the last term.

"Passing out."

"Oh."

"I don't know what else to tell you," Blake said. "I do want to know why we're both restrained and why we can't see our parents. That seems a bit...extreme to me."

"You're lying," Quinn said sharply.

"I am?" Victor said, astonished.

"Yeah. The doctor told us they had to defibrillate us, *twice*. They also had to *innovate* us so we could breathe."

"I think you mean intubate," Victor interjected.

Quinn nodded. "Yeah, that. We've also been here three or four days, which means *something* happened to us."

"Ah, yes, apologies. It's all a matter of perspective, I suppose. You weren't treated for anything because you were resuscitated after you both went into cardiac arrest shortly after arriving in the ER. The defibrillators reacted strangely, which is why I was called in."

"And you were called in because...?" Blake asked.

"I'm a local scientist and technical expert of sorts. I also love strange phenomena. When something strange or unusual happens, I get called in as the resident paranormal expert."

"With the armed guards outside the room, too?" Blake said, challenging the obvious lie Victor was feeding them.

"A precaution, to be sure. When the defibrillators fired, a bright blast of energy exploded between the two of you." Victor put his feet down and leaned forward. "I don't know about you, but I find that very strange and unusual."

"You're not going to tell us you see dead people and this is really the plot of *The Sixth Sense*, right?" Quinn asked.

Victor burst out laughing and slapped his right hand on his thigh. "No, of course not." He clapped his hands and regained his composure. "Wow, I've never heard that one before. That was great. You're funny, Quinn."

"Thanks."

"Speaking of strange and unusual, it's time for another test."

Quinn and Blake looked at each other and shrugged. He walked over to the counter space across from their beds and picked up a metal box with several silver rods sticking out from—the way Victor held it—the top of it. Quinn was about to ask him what it was, but Victor cut him off.

"So, you boys don't remember the thunderstorm Sunday morning?"

Quinn and Blake looked at each other again, then shook their heads.

"Huh?" Quinn uttered.

"There was a crazy storm *Saturday* night that knocked down all those trees we were following," Blake stated.

"There were several storms that night," Victor said. "You don't remember?"

"There was one," Blake said.

Victor shook his head. "There were three. Only one tracked over the campground."

"Wouldn't we have heard the other thunderstorms?"

"Do you sleep through thunderstorms at home?" Victor asked. He aimed the silver rods of the device at Blake, then swung it toward Quinn, who furled his eyebrows with concern and confusion.

"Yeah, I do. What is that thing?" Blake asked.

"Maybe you slept through the other storms, then. Sunday morning, a non-threatening thunderhead rolled through as the humidity increased. It was mainly heat lightning, which is of course difficult to see in the bright morning sunlight. Still, you should have noticed the lack of sun in the woods, you know, with the cloud cover and the natural darkness from tree shadows." Victor stepped between their beds and pointed the device at Blake, who made a face at it.

"I asked you what that was," Blake said, irritated.

"Oh, this little thing?" Victor asked, raising it a little. "This detects electrical currents in organic tissue."

"So I'm electrical now?" Blake asked.

Victor chuckled. "Of course. You were electrical before and you are electrical now. Human beings—and all animals, for that matter—are fascinating electrical organisms. Your brain sends and receives thousands of electrical signals every day. If we weren't electrical, a Taser would be ineffective."

He has a point.

Victor swung the device over to Quinn. "I think, filling in the gaps of your story and corroborating it with the unusual atmospheric conditions, you might have been close to a lightning strike that adversely affected you."

"We got struck by lightning?" Quinn exclaimed, trying to sit up again. The restraints held him back. *Dammit, these are annoying.*

"No, not struck by, but it's possible you were very close to one that obviously affected you."

Victor lowered the device and smiled. "All right, boys. I'm going to give you a little time to relax. You've been through a lot, so try to rest. I'm sure I won't be the first person to tell you that today."

Quinn spoke up. "But—"

"I'll be back, I promise," Victor said, raising an open palm to silence Quinn. "I need to check in right now. Rest up." Then he set the device on the counter and headed out of the room.

Quinn watched the door shut behind him, then he turned to his best friend. "He's lying to us," Quinn said.

"We're lying to him," Blake countered.

Quinn looked at his shackled wrists and the leather cuff restraints that held them in place. A similar set of cuffs held his ankles in place; each was connected by a strap that ran under his body. Any attempt to pull himself up used his own body weight against him. "We shouldn't be restrained like this. Something doesn't add up."

"No kidding," Blake answered. "I can't even scratch my nose."

"You think we're being watched?" Quinn whispered.

Blake nodded. "Camera over the door and another in the corner near the window."

Quinn looked in both spots and saw the familiar black bubble, indicating a security camera was present.

"I just assume the room is bugged, too."

Quinn smiled and looked at his friend. "Yup, we watch too much TV. Still, I noticed how uptight Victor seemed when he first walked into the room. Then he relaxed and sorta had fun with us as we told him the story."

"Yeah?"

"Yeah, but he was *too* relaxed with us, like he was trying really hard to be cool. I don't trust him."

"I don't think he's *that* bad."

Quinn shook his wrists in frustration. "Call me crazy, but I want to go back home and go back to school. Our friends must be wondering what the heck is going on with us."

"If they even know we're here. Seems pretty hush-hush to me," Blake commented. Then he smirked at Quinn. "You just want to see Keegan again."

"Maybe," Quinn said, blushing a little.

The door popped open, and Dr. Madison entered the room with Nurse Nadia, who shut the door behind them.

"Seriously, Doc," Quinn snapped, "where the hell are my dads?"

Dr. Madison smiled and raised her hands in surrender. "They're on their way. Your parents, too, Blake. We've just told them you're both awake. They've been staying at a local hotel."

"You mean they haven't been to see us yet?"

"No, remember, I told you they weren't allowed to see you."

"But we have rights. My dad's a lawyer. How did you keep him out?"

Dr. Madison looked at the closed door and grabbed the chart from the foot of Quinn's bed. Then she stepped in between the boys' beds and casually flipped through the chart and spoke with a low voice. "There are two cameras watching us. I don't think they record audio, but I'm not sure. Remember what I told you before Victor walked in; strange things happened while you were unconscious. Quinn, things around you moved all by themselves. Blake, the temperature on your side of the room inexplicably fluctuated between cold and hot. A few things levitated around both of you."

"Okay," Quinn whispered. "So, what is this Wilhelm Reich Museum he works at then?"

"It's an old orgone energy observatory. It's named after the famous Austrian psychoanalyst who lived there. To be honest, I'm not sure what they do, but they get involved whenever something unusual or paranormal happens around here. They have some kind of federal authority and autonomy, which is how they've kept your parents out."

Blake sighed. "I'm surprised my parents are even here."

"And we're tied up because…?"

"Because we didn't have enough information about what happened to you. Remember, you both died and we took some serious steps to bring you back and keep you alive. When the unusual phenomena started happening, there were too many unknowns."

"Right," Quinn said. "I guess that thunderstorm on Sunday morning really messed us up."

"Sunday morning?" Dr. Madison said, returning the medical chart to its holster on the foot of Quinn's bed. "There was no storm Sunday morning. Just that big one that came through late Saturday night."

"Oh, right," Quinn said. "I thought there was another storm."

"Nope. Okay, I'm going to go speak with Victor again. I believe the restraints can come off, but given the situation, I need to double-check with him."

"Thanks."

"Doctor?" Blake asked.

"Yes, Blake?"

"I need to pee."

Chapter 7

Organized Chaos

Blake

Two male nursing assistants, identified as Arik and Miguel on their name tags, unshackled Blake's wrist and ankle restraints. They lowered the bed rails and stepped aside as Blake swung his legs over the side of the bed, pulling his hospital gown down over his crotch.

"Sorry, buddy, but you ain't gonna like this part," Arik said. "We have to watch you pee." He was about five and a half feet tall and spent most of his time in the gym lifting weights. He sported a buzz cut and a few tattoos.

"What?" Blake exclaimed. *You've got to be kidding me.*

"Trust me, it's not my choice, but orders are orders."

Quinn giggled in the bed next to him.

"What are you laughing at, sunshine?" Miguel said, the taller, bearded man with glasses and styled, messy hair, a wide grin on his face. "You're next."

"Oh," Quinn said, his face dropping.

Blake stood and winked at Quinn. He slipped his feet into some hospital slippers and tried to hold his gown closed behind him with his left hand as he crossed the room. When he entered the bathroom, he didn't care about his nakedness. He fumbled with the gown because it awkwardly draped across his front and he didn't know how to pee standing up with it in the way.

"Just hike it up and tuck it between your left side and arm. There's no fancy way to do this, believe me," Arik offered.

"You want me to stand in front of you, almost naked, and pee?" Blake asked, glaring at the nurse's aide. *Okay, maybe I do care about being naked now.*

"No, not at all, but my boss does, and I'd rather not get fired today. Besides, it's not like you're the first naked dude I've seen, not that I'm bragging. It just comes with the territory." He nodded toward the toilet and pointed at it with his finger. "Just aim it well and pretend I'm not even here." Then he stepped back and leaned against the sink, folding his arms across his chest.

Blake sighed and closed his eyes. *Running streams, babbling brooks, flowing fountains, ocean waves, dripping water…* When the urge finally came, he opened his eyes and aimed.

A minute later, he finished up and let the gown fall. Arik checked the toilet before Blake flushed it and then stepped aside so he could use the sink. "Well, at least it's the right color."

"Did you expect my pee to be neon pink or something?" Blake asked, washing his hands.

"Not at all, just had to make sure there was no blood in your urine."

"Oh. Well, I hope that was all that and more for you," Blake quipped, glad the experience was over.

"I can die in peace now," Arik joked back. "Next!"

"Wait, he doesn't get a turn, too?" Blake asked, pointing to Miguel.

"Nah, not today. I won Rock, Paper, Scissors before we came in."

"That's how you decided who gets to watch the golden stream?" Quinn asked.

Miguel shrugged. "I never said it was a thrilling decision."

Quinn, holding his gown closed behind him and shuffling along in his hospital slippers, made his way into the bathroom to do his business as Blake walked over to the window, his gown flapping open behind him, not wanting to crawl back in bed and get tied down again. Outside, trees swayed in a gentle breeze as the sun shone brightly in the sky.

The door to their room popped open, and Blake grabbed his gown and spun around, unsure of whom he was mooning. *Oh, it's you.*

Victor poked his head in and stepped into the room and surveyed the situation. He winced when he saw Arik standing near Quinn in the bathroom. He looked over at Miguel, who patiently waited for Blake to lie down again so he could restrain him. He raised his hand and spoke to Miguel and Arik. "Just spoke with Dr. Madison. Please remove the restraints from their beds."

"Sure thing," Miguel said.

"Boys, your parents are signing in downstairs. They'll be up momentarily."

"Oh sure," Quinn called out from the bathroom, "Remove the restraint things before our parents get here, right?"

Victor smirked. "Something like that." Then he looked at Arik. "Is he peeing green?"

Arik frowned and shook his head. "No, of course not."

"He's fine then, thank you for following orders."

"You're good, champ," Arik said, clapping Quinn on the shoulder and leaving him to do his business. He walked over to Quinn's bed and unfastened the restraints.

"Here's a tip," Miguel said, reaching into one of the closets. He tossed Blake a second hospital gown and set one on Quinn's bed. "Put the second gown on like a bathrobe so your backside is covered. This way you won't give any old ladies a thrill or a heart attack if you step out of your room."

"Thanks." Blake smiled and put the bathrobe on backwards, cinching it in the front.

When Arik and Miguel finished removing the restraints from their beds, they left the room and shut the door behind them. Victor followed them out. Blake noticed the armed guards were no longer standing outside the room.

Quinn walked out of the bathroom and pulled on the second hospital gown, covering his backside from view. Then, he joined Blake at the window and looked at the scenery outside.

"They said things were levitating around us," Quinn said. He turned around and extended his hand toward the chart in the footboard holster. "Rise."

Nothing happened.

"You try."

"Are you serious?" Blake asked.

"Just do it."

"Fine." Blake looked at the medical chart and extended his hand. He pictured it floating in his mind. "Go up."

Nothing happened for him, either.

"Damn," Quinn said. "Things moved around me, and the room temperature got hot and cold around you." He whipped his head around and looked into Blake's eyes. Then he reached out and grabbed Blake's arms.

"How do you feel now? Are you hot or cold?"

"I think I'm fine, but the air conditioning in here is a bit on the cold side to me."

Quinn dropped his hands. He made pouty lips and took a deep breath. "Yeah, it's chilly in here to me as well, and your temperature feels normal to me."

Blake turned and pointed to the medical whiteboards on the wall opposite their beds. "Well, according to our vitals, our temperatures are normal."

"True," Quinn said. "I just thought, maybe…"

A moment of silence passed before Blake urged him on. "Maybe what?"

"Maybe we got superpowers or something."

Blake burst out laughing. "Yeah, right."

"Rise!" Quinn exclaimed, turning quickly and extending his hand toward the medical chart once more.

Nothing.

Then he turned back to Blake and whispered to him. "I know we can't talk about it here, but something definitely happened to us. All that swirly blue stuff—it's like in us now or something. Wait…" Quinn turned and looked at the counter space opposite their beds, under the whiteboards.

"You're kidding," Blake said, racing over to the counter with Quinn. Together, they stared at the device Victor had used on them. "What do you think it does?"

Quinn picked it up and turned it right side up so the writing wasn't upside down. "Orgone Energy Detector," he read aloud. "What the hell is orgone energy?"

"Beats me. Turn it on. See what it does."

"Yeah!" Quinn flipped the switch and pointed it at Blake. The digital three-inch band of thirty or so small LEDs spread across the top of the device illuminated from left to right, from green to yellow to red. Under the LEDs, printed labels offered the words *Low, Concentration,* and *High.* A larger LED above the word *High* flashed red.

"Oh, I get it. Low or high concentration," Quinn said. He turned to the right, away from Blake, and all the LEDs turned off except the first green one.

"That's weird."

"What did it do?" Blake said, stepping next to Quinn to see the face of the meter.

"As soon as I pointed it away from you, the little lights turned off."

"Maybe it was booting up. Aim it at me again."

Quinn aimed the meter at Blake's stomach so Blake could see the lights. As soon as the meter's sensor pointed at Blake, all the LEDs, including the big, flashing red one, switched on again.

Quinn aimed the device at the wall: only one green light. He handed the meter to Blake. "Do me."

Blake studied the face of the meter, but it offered no further explanation of what it did. He took a deep breath and pointed it at Quinn. Once more, all the LEDs, including the flashing red one, switched on.

"Wicked," Blake said, exhaling. "Does this mean we're...full of ozone?"

"Orgone," Quinn corrected. "I'd say yes."

"Holy crap." Blake set the device back on the counter and backed away from it. "What does that mean? Why does he have this meter thing and the hospital doesn't? Is it like...radiation?"

"I don't feel sick, so it's not likely to be nuclear radiation. I think our innards would've been turned to soup by now. Maybe it takes longer, I don't know." Quinn pointed at the door. "If we were a radiation hazard, they'd be coming in here with yellow hazmat suits and all that stuff. I'm willing to bet Victor saw this same high concentration readout...but he didn't freak out. So we don't seem to be in any foreseeable danger, not that I'd know what foreseeable danger accompanies this thing that happened to us."

"Except now we're full of this orgone stuff. If I had my phone, I could Google it."

"Should we tell our parents?" Quinn asked in a low voice.

"What, that we wandered into a mystery cave and got blasted with…orgone?" Blake whispered. "Heck no. I don't want to be grounded for the rest of my life."

"Right, and I don't want to admit anything in here just in case our friend Victor is listening."

A knock at the door startled them, and they turned around. Blake saw Nadia's face smiling at them. "Goodness, they are up. Go ahead and see your boys."

She pushed the door wide open, and Blake saw Quinn's dads standing in the doorway. Their faces conveyed exhaustion, panic, and worry, and Dad hadn't shaved in several days. Daddio clapped his hands over his mouth as tears streamed down his face. Quinn rushed to them, and they met in the middle of the room for a giant hug.

Blake smiled.

Then his parents, Stella and Ralph, walked in. His mother's face looked worried, but his father's face looked angry and annoyed. His hands were stuffed into the pockets of his cargo shorts. When he made eye contact with Blake, he grunted and didn't smile.

"Blake," his mother said, walking quickly across the room. Blake took a few steps forward but stopped when she got to him first. She grabbed his hands and smiled through tears that threatened her mascara. "Are you all right? You look all right to me."

"I'm fine, Mom."

"They told us you were struck by lightning, is that true?" Stella asked.

"I guess so," Blake said, looking over at Quinn's family hug. His mom pulled him in for a hug and kissed him on the cheek. She stepped back and turned to look at his father, who hadn't moved from his spot near the door.

Ralph pulled his hands out of his pockets and crossed his arms across his chest. His eyes narrowed. "It's Thursday. I've lost four days of work because of you. What the hell did you do to keep us—"

"I don't know, Dad," Blake snapped, his hands balling into fists. "They told us we were caught in a thunderstorm and might have been struck by lightning."

"Don't use that tone of voice with me, mister. You're in enough trouble as it is."

"For what? I didn't do anything wrong!"

"There was *no* thunderstorm on Sunday morning," Daddio said, redirecting the conversation. Quinn's parents stopped their family hug and turned to face Blake and his mom. Daddio kept his arm around Quinn's shoulders. "I kept telling the doctor that, but they couldn't explain what happened to you or why your hearts stopped beating. They kept saying your symptoms were consistent with a lightning strike, with the exception of no burns on your bodies."

Blake looked down at his arms and bare feet. *No burns. That's weird, our doctor agreed there was no thunderstorm on Sunday morning.*

"What's the doctor's name again?" Blake asked.

"Doctor Kraze," Dad said. "Sounds like an evil villain name, if you ask me."

Quinn looked over at Blake with a confused expression on his face.

Blake shrugged. "Um, our doctor's name is Amy Madison."

"Yeah, today it is. Dr. Kraze is off today," Stella said.

"Oh," Blake said softly. *This is getting confusing.*

"Could it have been food poisoning?" Quinn offered sheepishly, looking up at Daddio.

His dads looked at each other and shrugged. "We ate the same burgers and stuff you did, and we're fine," Daddio said.

"It's a good thing other people were out hiking that day," Dad added. "You could have been unconscious on the forest floor for a long time. We wouldn't have thought anything of it until lunch time, or maybe later, when it was too late."

"What were you doing in the woods?" Ralph asked, annoyance grating in his voice.

"We were following the hiking trail until we came across a bunch of fallen trees that went on for a while. We just decided to follow them out. When we came back, we passed out on the trail."

"What a wimp," Ralph muttered under his breath.

Dad shot him an angry look and shook his head.

A knock at the door turned everyone's heads. Nurse Nadia entered, her face full of joy and a wide grin. "Hello, happy families." In her hands, she carried two blue plastic bags that said *Personal Belongings* in large white text.

"It is a good day because you get to go home today."

"Finally," Ralph said, stepping aside to let Nadia through.

"These are the clothes you had on when you arrived. Mister Blake, your cell phone is in here too."

"Great," Blake said, stepping forward to take his bag from Nadia. She handed Quinn his bag of clothes.

"But no cell phone for you, Mister Quinn. I hope it is not lost."

"We have it in the car," Daddio said. "He didn't take it with him when he went hiking."

"Oh, such wonderful news for you, Mister Quinn. I was worried it was lost."

Blake found his cell phone and switched it on, but nothing happened. "It doesn't work."

"Battery's probably dead," Daddio offered. "We have your clean clothes in the car if you guys want those."

"Nah," Blake said. "These are fine. They don't look dirty or anything. I can't stand another minute in this hospital dress."

"Me neither," Quinn said, laughing.

"All right then, you guys get changed and we'll get you discharged at the desk."

"There goes our insurance deductible," Ralph said. Then he turned around and walked toward the door.

"Okay then, happy parents, come and follow me to the desk and we'll get you ready to go home with your boys." Nadia smiled at the boys and gestured with her hands for the parents to follow her out of the room.

When they had left, Blake tossed his bag onto his bed and sorted through his clothes. Shorts, boxers, tank top, socks, and his sneakers. He pulled off his hospital gowns and pulled on his boxers. Quinn did the same at his bed, and the boys got dressed.

"This is all fucked up," Blake said. "I don't understand why there's so much lying and covering up in this hospital. Why did Victor pretend to be a doctor to our parents?"

"Unless he lied to us," Quinn said, snapping the elastic waistband of his boxers against his abs. "Maybe he really is a doctor."

Blake reached for his shorts. "Wearing a black suit and not a doctor's lab coat?"

"Good point. What if everything he told us was a lie?" Quinn speculated. "What if Dr. Madison and Victor are in this together, and they both work for that paranormal museum place?" He pulled on his tank top and sat on the edge of the bed to put on his socks.

Blake thought about the possibility for a moment and then reached for his tank top. "I think Victor was mostly honest with us, but not honest with our parents." He sat down on the edge of his bed, facing Quinn, and reached for his socks. "I also think Dr. Madison was partly honest with us."

"But they each had different stories," Quinn argued. "Victor got to our parents first. If he really is part of some super-secret conspiracy theory, doesn't it make sense that he did all the lying because he's the one trying to figure out what really happened to us?"

"Maybe," Blake said.

"And look," Quinn said, pointing at the orgone meter with the sneaker he held in his hand. "That thing is still here, and the hospital people haven't bothered to notice it or remove it."

"So?"

"Too sloppy. Victor didn't accidentally leave it here. He purposefully left it here, knowing we'd play with it. He knew we'd be too damn curious about what it was once he used it on us. He didn't answer any of our questions, and there's a *reason* he wants us to know that he knows we went into that cave thing. I just don't know why."

"You think he's telling us something?" Blake said, tying his sneaker laces.

"Definitely."

"Should we take it with us?"

"No," Quinn said, smiling wickedly. "I think he expects us to take it. I say we leave it here and mess with *his* head this time."

Victor

Victor Kraze walked into the empty hospital room previously occupied by Quinn and Blake. He looked around, hoping to find something out of place or unusual.

Nothing.

His eyes landed on the orgone meter, and he walked over to it, the corner of his mouth forming a smile. When he'd set it down earlier, the sensor had faced the window. Now, the sensor faced the door, which meant the boys had played with it.

Excellent...

Chapter 8
Altered

Quinn

Quinn blinked his blue eyes in the morning light and yawned. He stretched and then rolled over, refusing to get up despite the bright sunlight shining in his eyes. A knock at the door startled him.

"Time to get up, son," Daddio said through the closed door.

"Yup," he called out. *Finally, things are back to normal.*

He pushed the covers down to his waist. He felt wetness around his legs and torso when he moved.

What the hell?

He sat up, looked around, and realized he had sweat during the night and the sheets were damp and clammy where he had lain.

Gross.

He got up and pulled the covers back so the bed would air out during the day. Tomorrow was Saturday, and he would be changing the bedding anyway.

He dropped to the floor and cranked out his pushups. At fifty, he flipped over and worked through one hundred crunches. When he finished, he collapsed to the floor, his breath momentarily sucked out of him as his abs recovered. Since he hadn't worked out in over a week, his abs burned and he struggled to breathe. He willed himself to sit up, bracing for the pain, but none came.

Huh, that's weird.

Quinn pushed himself off the floor and flexed in the mirror over his dresser. Then he grabbed his towel from behind the bedroom door and made his way to the bathroom across the hall.

Quinn relaxed his body under the hot stream of water, letting it soothe his muscles. He closed his eyes and thought about the strange interview with Victor Kraze and the flurry of lies that surrounded what happened to them in the mystery cave and the Sunday morning weather. He became frustrated when his mind replayed and overanalyzed the events that put him and Blake into the hospital.

If only we'd never found that damn tunnel entrance.

Quinn opened his eyes.

What the hell?

In the shower, drops of water hovered in front of him as the stream of shower water continued to flow. He looked more carefully and watched as water droplets splashed off his body and the shower walls. Instead of falling toward his feet and the drain, they remained suspended in midair. He raised his hand, and some of the droplets moved upward.

His eyes opened wide and his mouth dropped open. He moved his left hand to his body, and some of the hovering water droplets, now collecting together into bigger drops, moved with him. With the fingers of his left hand, he flicked water off his chest, and the drops moved away from him, slowing to a stop and defying gravity.

Wicked. Am I doing this?

He looked at the flowing stream of water running down over his body, and he moved his right hand toward it.

Bend the stream.

As his hand approached the stream, it bent where his hand was and angled away from its normal path.

No way…

He turned his hand palm-side up, and the water reversed direction, spraying the tile ceiling above him. "Oh crap," he exclaimed, dropping his hand. The shower stream resumed its normal path toward the floor. All at once, the floating water drops rained to the shower floor with a big splashing sound.

I don't believe I just did that. How did I just do that?

Surprise and wonder filled his mind as he raised his hand again. This time, the water did not move.

Oh come on, seriously? Wait, I know…bend the stream.

As his hand approached the stream, nothing happened.

Dammit! What the heck happened? Come on, Quinn, you can do this…bend the stream.

He stepped back and raised both hands to the stream. All at once, the shower stream redirected to the wall.

Yes!

He moved his hands, and again the stream moved with him. He raised his right hand up and lowered his left hand; the shower stream curved between his hands before splashing near the drain.

Quinn thought about the floating water again and focused his mind. As the stream continued to flow in between his hands in a curve, floating water drops began expanding from the stream and all the water collecting on the floor of the shower stall floated upward.

Now, make one giant ball of water…

As Quinn thought about it, the water began amassing at the center of the shower between his hands, the flow of water changing its course to fill an imaginary round container in front of him.

I wonder if I can Hadouken this water…but to where?

Quinn looked around the shower. *Just a little push…to the wall.*

He brought his hands closer to his body, and the orb of water moved toward him.

Hadouken!

He pushed his hands forward a little and imagined a gentle blast of water moving forward. The water responded, but with more gusto than he anticipated. The giant orb of water exploded on the wall in front of him and splashed downward to the floor. Then, the shower stream resumed its normal course.

So, does this make me Aquaman now?

"Remind me, you have track practice after school today, right?" Dad asked, pulling into the school parking lot.

"Yup." Quinn gestured to the gym bag in the back seat.

"That's right, sorry. My mind's still freaked out about this past week. You're super sure you want to go to school today?"

"Definitely," Quinn said. "I don't want to be cooped up any more."

"I hear ya." Dad stopped the car and smiled at his son. "Give us a hug."

Quinn leaned over and hugged his father. "See you tonight, Dad." Then he grabbed his backpack and gym bag from the back seat and shut the door, waving to his dad as he walked toward the school building.

"Hey, Quinn!" someone yelled out. "Welcome back."

Quinn looked up and waved. It was Joe, from the track team. "Thanks, man," Quinn yelled back.

"Quinn!" a familiar voice called out. It was Ravone. Quinn waved and jogged over to the bench she and Loren were sitting on. She stood up and extended her arms toward him. He dropped his gym bag on the ground and wrapped his arms around her.

"What the hell kind of trouble have you been up to?" Ravone asked. "Wait, you're okay, right? Oh, never mind. I'm just glad to have you back in one piece."

"Um, I can't wait to tell you, and yes," Quinn said, smiling.

They stopped hugging, and Loren stood up to hug him as well. "Your dads called our parents and told us you were in the hospital."

"Oh boy," Quinn said, hugging Loren. He let go and sat down in between Loren and Ravone.

"So are you an official lightning strike survivor?" Loren asked.

"Wait," Ravone said. "Blake's back too, right? He's just not here yet?"

"Yeah, he's back," Quinn said, looking around. "He's probably just late or something. And, uh, the honest answer is, we don't know about the lightning strike. Something definitely happened, though." *I need to talk to Blake first about whether we talk about the tunnel and the cave thing or keep it quiet.*

"We did our homework," Ravone said, briefly waving her phone. "There was a freak thunderstorm with a microburst that touched down not far from the campground you guys were staying at. That must have been so scary!"

"On Saturday night? Yeah, totally. We took shelter in my dad's SUV until the storm passed. It was pretty quick, actually. The next morning, we saw a bunch of downed trees on the other side of the campground. No one got hurt, but it could have been a bad scene."

"Oh my gosh!" Loren exclaimed.

"Yeah," Quinn said, "I know, right? They could have fallen on us. Anyway, Blake and I decided to go exploring, and we found some hiking trails. On the trail we took, we saw a whole row of pine trees knocked down, and we followed them into the woods. When we came back, we never made it to the campground. Apparently, a family found us unconscious on the trail, and that's how we ended up in the hospital for several days."

"Wow," Ravone said, shaking her head. "Is it true what your dad said? That you guys actually died and the doctors had to resuscitate you?"

Quinn nodded. "That's what they told us."

"That's so cool," Loren said, smiling. Then, his face expressed sadness. "I mean, that's terrible."

"I know what you mean," Quinn said, laughing. "Out of curiosity, when you were checking up on the weather, did you see any weather reports for Sunday morning?"

"Not really," Ravone said. "It looked like it was mostly sunny with pockets of rain here in the northern parts of New Hampshire and Maine."

"Oh, okay, I just—" Quinn slapped the side of his head with his right hand as a loud noise echoed in his ears. "What the hell is that?"

"What's what?" Loren asked, looking at Ravone with confusion.

"You don't hear that loud noise?"

"No," Ravone said, looking around.

Suddenly, Quinn was overwhelmed with a strong sense of proximity to Blake. Specifically, he saw in his mind that Blake was fifty feet to his left and walking toward him. Except now, Blake had stopped walking and squatted, cradling his head in both hands. Quinn looked out and confirmed with his eyes what his mind told him.

Holy shit, I can sense you.

Quinn watched Blake shake his head as the sensation faded for both boys. Blake stood, looked around, and continued walking toward the group, shooting Quinn a worried look.

Ravone got up and jogged toward Blake, shouting something about him being okay.

"They should just date," Loren said.

Quinn slapped his thigh and laughed. "Uh, I think poor Ravone is going to find herself in a tragic Shakespearean stage play of unrequited love."

"Oh, I know, but she's already there. It was worth a shot, though."

Blake and Ravone joined Quinn and Loren on the bench.

"Hey, Blake," Quinn said, "I was just telling the gals here about our adventure."

"Oh?" Blake said, sounding concerned.

"Yeah, I was telling them what *Doctor Victor* told our parents about the Sunday morning thunderstorms and how no one's really sure if we got struck by lightning or not."

"Oh, right, that," Blake said, looking relieved.

"Don't worry, we'll have time to catch up, right?" Quinn asked, raising his eyebrows, hoping Blake caught the message.

"Yes," Blake answered, nodding slowly.

"Hey, Quinn," a sexy voice said.

Whoa!

Quinn turned and saw Keegan standing there, shirtless and holding his longboard in his left hand.

"Hi," Quinn said, his voice pitching much higher than he expected.

"Hey, Blake. Heard you guys were in the hospital this week. Glad you're okay. Nothing serious, I hope?"

"Nothing serious if you don't consider surviving a lightning strike serious," Loren commented.

Blake rolled his eyes and chuckled.

"Really?" Keegan asked, eyes wide.

"Well, we don't really know, but it might have been that, yeah," Blake said.

"Wow. I want to say that's awesome, but that seems really awkward to say at the moment." Keegan replied.

"I get it," Quinn said, smiling. Some confidence found its way into his mind. "I'll tell you about it later if you want."

The three heads of Blake, Ravone, and Loren snapped to attention and then turned to Keegan.

Keegan slowly nodded. "Sure. Gotta go for now, though. Bye."

"Bye," Quinn said, raising a hand to wave as the wheels of Keegan's longboard clacked down onto the pavement. Seconds later, Keegan was gone.

Quinn felt his eyes pop open as he turned his head to face his friends. He squealed with delight and clapped his hands. His friends laughed with him.

Finally. My crush knows I exist.

Quinn approached the library doors. He stumbled when a sudden, loud ringing echoed in his ears, similar to the one he'd felt earlier that morning. He grabbed at his temples with the palms of both hands. Then, he sensed exactly where Blake sat in the library. A moment later, the sensation abated, and he walked into the library to look for Blake. Sure enough, Blake sat where he expected, lowering his hands from his head.

They had agreed to meet during their free period to discuss the morning's unexpected sensory event. The table Blake sat at was secluded, and they could chat in private without other students overhearing them. He sat down and pulled out his biology textbook and notebook to make it look like he was studying.

"Hey," Blake said, shaking his head. "That's annoying."

"Hi," Quinn answered. "No kidding, but we'll get to that in a second. The first thing we need to be on the same page about is the story we tell people, right? So are we good with the mystery lightning storm and not ever talking about the underground stuff?"

Blake nodded. "Totally. I realized last night we didn't get a chance to sync up about our *story*. There's already enough confusion around it, officially, at least. Besides, I don't want anyone knowing what we did."

"I know, right? Someone else might not survive that ordeal."

"I wasn't even thinking about that."

"Oh, okay. All right, secondly, you felt or heard—not sure which—that thing in your head when you got near me this morning? And just now before I walked into the library?"

Blake leaned forward. "Yes, how freaky was that? This morning, I knew exactly where you were and how far away you were from me. I even knew, for like a split second, that you were feeling the same pain I was. Just now, I knew you were walking in here."

"Ditto for me. I knew exactly where you were, too. We're gonna have to test this one out. This is apparently our second superpower."

"Wait, what?"

"We have superpowers now."

"*Powers?*" Blake said, emphasizing the plurality of the word.

"Yeah…you know, this morning in the shower, did you…?"

"Well, yeah, but I do that all the time."

"What?" Quinn asked, staring blankly at Blake.

"You know," Blake answered, gesturing with his hand.

"Oh!" Quinn said. "Right, but that's not at all what I'm talking about."

"Uh…you've lost me, then."

"The water. The thing with the water. Do you have the water *superpower?*" Blake slowly shook his head.

Quinn leaned in. "The water didn't float in the shower?"

Blake shook his head again, his face awash with confusion. He leaned forward and whispered, "What are you talking about?"

"Oh man, you will, I know you will. Unless…our powers are different. Whoa, that would really make us a dynamic duo."

"Stop, just stop. I am not the Robin to your Batman, no matter what's going on. Take a deep breath and explain to me what this water power is."

"Okay…" Quinn took a deep breath and explained the water phenomenon he'd experienced in the shower. Blake's eyes widened with surprise and then disappointment as Quinn finished his story. "And then I could control it. I don't know why or how…but I could."

"I didn't do anything magical in the shower."

"Huh, that's weird."

"If you get powers and I don't, I'll be pissed."

"Well, you can sense me. So that's good sign."

"You can sense me, that's a good sign," Darien jeered, glaring at them as he walked by their table. Blake glared back at him and they watched him go, but not before Darien flipped them the bird and called out, "Losers" at a level much too loud for the library.

"What a jerk," Quinn said. "I want to punch him out so bad."

Blake smiled and whispered to Quinn. "Wait, can you get him all wet or something?"

"I would need water, and I don't know. I don't fully understand how to control it yet."

Two periods later, Quinn sat in the fourth row of physics class. A few seats over, Keegan Miller took notes as Mr. St. Germain, one of Quinn's favorite teachers, explained the principles of fluid mechanics, a startlingly on-point topic Quinn took no interest in. Instead, he gazed at the back of Keegan's head and daydreamed of an imaginary first date in Prescott Park with Keegan.

"Did you want to kiss me tonight?" Keegan asked.

Quinn felt the blood rush to his cheeks. "Yes," he answered sheepishly. "Of course."

"Good, because I've wanted to kiss you for a long time now."

"Really?"

"Yeah, really," Keegan said, shifting closer to Quinn on the lawn blanket they had brought to the park. "I've always thought you were cute. I didn't think you liked me, though. I'm glad I was wrong."

Their thighs touched and Quinn could barely contain his excitement—and nervousness.

"Me too," Quinn said. Then he stared into the piercing blue eyes looking back at him and smiled.

"So," Keegan said, blushing a little and running his hand through his hair.

"Yeah?" Quinn said.

Keegan chuckled and shuffled closer again. Now, their shoulders were touching.

Quinn leaned forward and met Keegan's lips.

Crash!

The sound of shattering glass snapped Quinn back to reality. At the same time, Mr. St. Germain stopped talking and looked at the back of the science room where the chemistry equipment was stored. The entire class and Quinn turned around to see what had happened. They all gasped softly when they saw several of the large 1,000 mL beakers on the top shelf had shattered. Pieces of glass were still falling between the shelves and the locked glass cabinets that prevented students from accessing the equipment without teacher supervision.

Oh crap, did I do that?

"Huh," Mr. St. Germain said. "Didn't expect that today."

"What just happened?" a girl asked at the back of the room.

Quinn sat back down and shrank into his chair.

I just happened, that's what.

Chapter 9

Testing the Waters

Blake

B lake's tired legs burned and begged him to stop running, but he couldn't give in. Less than a mile away, the school track field signaled the end of another grueling run Coach had sent the team on around Portsmouth. Several days away from running, while laid up in the hospital, had softened up his endurance, but he was determined to get it back. He felt aggravated by his not-so-thrilling performance because he didn't like finishing with the last group. Despite his fatigue, he thought he sensed a newfound strength bubbling up inside him that encouraged him to finish strong. He had never felt this before...or maybe his muscles weren't as soft as he thought.

Several hundred feet behind him, Quinn was being dramatic about dying and losing the will to live. Blake chuckled.

Five minutes later, Blake turned onto Andrew Jarvis Drive, the street that would take him to the high school campus and its athletic fields. Someone leaving the campus shouted, "Go Clippers" and beeped their car horn at him. He absentmindedly waved as he ran through the nearby parking lot between him and the track field.

That's when he noticed someone running toward him. "What's up, champ?" Darien called out. He started jogging alongside Blake. "You're all super sweaty today."

Oh come on, I don't need your shit today.

"Hey," Blake said, breathing heavily as his eyes focused on the gates to Clippers Field. He glanced down and saw the sweat glistening on his torso and arms. He could feel beads of sweat rolling down the shirtless skin of his back, chest, and sides. His running shorts were soaked, and the sweat dripped to the ground from his elbows. *Good grief, why am I such a sweaty mess today?*

"Glad to see you are still able to run after your little siesta in the woods. I wish my daddies would take me out of school to go on a vacation."

Blake rolled his eyes. "Shut up, Darien," he said through huffs. *If we weren't on school grounds I'd clock you good right now.*

"Aww, what's the matter? Are you out of breath?"

Blake shrugged. "So what? The sun's hot today. Also, I haven't run for a week." It was a hot day, probably one of the last few until the spring, but it wasn't like running in the middle of the summer.

"I guess when you take almost a full week off from school to go camping with your boyfriend, you can't—"

Blake snarled and abruptly stopped running in the middle of the parking lot and grabbed Darien's right arm at the biceps, jerking him to a standstill. "He's not my—"

"Ouch! Jesus Christ!" Darien yelled. He wrenched his arm free from Blake's grip. "Don't squeeze so hard, that fucking burned!" Surprised, Blake looked at Darien's arm and noted a red imprint where his hand had grabbed Darien's bicep.

"You deserve it, you little shit," Blake said angrily.

Darien winced and backed up. "Wow, you're hot."

"What is your problem now?" Blake exclaimed, confused. *You're not gay, or are you?*

"You're *hot*, like you're on fire or something. I can feel the heat coming off your body." Darien lightly tapped at his arm where Blake's hand had grabbed him.

What are you talking about?

"You're such a freak, Hargreaves," Darien said, backing away toward the field where the rest of the team was stretching and cooling down. "You and your little boyfriend Quinn the Queer."

Blake's hands balled into fists and tightened. He took a step forward and then grabbed the side of his head with his hands as an overwhelming sense of proximity to Quinn echoed in his mind. Blake turned around to confirm what his mind told him, that Quinn was jogging toward him on the other side of the parking lot. Quinn's hands moved toward his head and he slowed to a stop, doubling over for a moment before jumping up and walking over to Blake.

"Freaks," Darien yelled. Blake turned his head and watched him run across the field.

"Hey," Quinn called out, clutching his side. Blake turned to look at his friend. Quinn's mouth fell open when he met Blake's gaze. "Oh my gosh!"

"What?" Blake asked.

Quinn looked around and grabbed Blake's arm. "Walk with me. Wow, you're hot." Quinn pulled him toward the edge of the parking lot where no one would see them.

"What's wrong?" Blake asked.

"Your eyes are glowing yellow-orange," Quinn said softly.

"What?" Blake said, blinking.

"Your eyes are *glowing*," Quinn repeated in a loud whisper.

Blake took a moment to sense his body. "I can feel something different behind my eyes."

"Turn them off, now!"

"I don't know how!"

"Okay, okay," Quinn said. "Just take a minute to breathe. Close your eyes and try to forget about Darien."

Blake felt power surge behind his eyes at the bully's name.

"Nope, not working," Quinn said. "Just got brighter. Calm thoughts, buddy, calm thoughts."

Blake nodded, closed his eyes, and took a deep breath. *I'm quiet, enjoying the beach, lying in the sun, relaxing...*

He opened his eyes and looked at Quinn, who now walked around him in a circle, needing to cool off and work his tired leg muscles.

"Better, much better," Quinn said softly.

"Good."

"Wow, okay, we're gonna have to be super careful about that glowing eyes trick. How'd you do on today's run?"

"Terrible," Blake answered. "Stupidly tough run today. It's like I had the strength but didn't at the same time."

"I know what you mean," Quinn said.

Blake noted Quinn was drenched in sweat as well.

"So, um, what did jerk-face want?" Quinn asked.

"He was up to no good. Just being an ass, that's all." *You don't need to know any more than that.*

"Did you get mad at him?

"Yeah, why?" *What are you getting at?*

Quinn pointed to the ground where he was still walking around Blake.

Blake looked down. He stood in the center of a six-foot black circle in the gray asphalt parking lot. The painted parking lines that intersected with the circle had turned dark gray.

"What about it?" Blake asked, looking up at Quinn.

"For starters, it's really warm near you, and the asphalt around you is smoking. It's...scorched in a perfect circle over where you two were fighting and also right here where you're standing."

Blake looked at the dark circles again. Sure enough, he stood in the center of a scorched and smoking piece of pavement. Blake stepped out of it quickly.

"I hope no one saw that." *Maybe that's why Darien was calling me a freak?*

"We might have just discovered your second superpower," Quinn whispered. "After the sensing thing, of course."

"Makes sense."

Quinn looked up and grinned. "What do you mean?"

Blake explained what happened with Darien. "And like, there's all this sweat pouring off me. You're pretty soaked, too."

"Yeah," Quinn answered, flicking sweat from his fingers. "I thought it was a little weird, but I assumed it's because it is hotter than normal and we hadn't run in a week. I'm gonna call you Scorched Earth."

"No, you're not," Blake said, chuckling. "Can you get out of the house tonight?"

"I'm working till close."

"Right. Um, how about after, then?"

"Yeah, I guess so. It's Friday, so I don't think my dads will care. Why?"

"Meet me on the back field after work."

"I'll be on my bike, so it will take a few minutes for me to get there, assuming we close on time."

"I'll be there."

"Okay, buddy."

Blake pedaled through the empty school grounds and made his way to the back baseball field. The weight of three gallons of water in his backpack pulled him down, and the straps of his backpack cut deep into his shoulder muscles. He smirked when he rolled over one of the charred pavement circles he'd probably caused in the afternoon. Then, as he rode around the football field on the track, he kept close to the tree line to avoid any security cameras. When he finally made it to the baseball field, no one else was around. Arriving at one of the dugouts, he quietly rested his bike against the backside of the dugout's painted wood and turned off the headlight and the blinking red rear light. He unstrapped his helmet and pulled off his backpack, glad to be rid of the weight. He walked into the dugout and set them down on the bench. Then he sat down next to them, rotating his helmet so it faced the field.

Then, he watched and waited.

Silence. *Good.*

Sometimes students would sneak into the ball fields to hang out, make out, or do other things Blake only heard stories about. He didn't want to be seen by other students, and if a patrol car swung through, he figured they'd have enough time to hide behind the dugout.

After a few minutes, when nothing moved and no signs of human life around the field made their presence known, Blake grabbed his backpack and walked across the sandy infield to the grass behind second base. When he got there, he set the backpack down and pulled out the three gallons of water, setting them down in a cluster. He opened each one and threw the caps into his backpack, which he set aside.

Since he felt warm, he pulled off his T-shirt and tucked it into the waistband of his shorts. Then he sat down cross-legged on the grass and faced the three gallons of water. He rested his elbows on his knees and his head on his hands.

So how does this work? Do I think about what I want you to do?

Float!

Go up!

Splash around!

Hmmm, that's not it.

Blake sighed. He raised his hand toward the water.

Maybe I have to pretend I'm a Jedi or something... Move.

Nothing. He laid back and felt the cool grass against his warm back and looked up at the stars through the cloudless night. Above him, the Northern Star and the Big and Little Dippers jumped out at him from the sea of starlight.

Blake winced at the now familiar but still overwhelming sense of proximity to Quinn echoing in his mind. To his left, the clicking sound of a bike wheel dragged his attention away from the constellations. He looked left and saw Quinn riding in.

Quinn pedaled closer and Blake sat up.

"Dammit," Quinn called out. "I forgot about that stupid sensing thing. Almost knocked me off my bike."

"Oh, yeah. Careful."

"Watchya doing?" Quinn asked.

"Stargazing and waiting for you."

"How romantic."

"Ha."

"Um, why do you have three gallons of water in the middle of the baseball field?"

"To watch you play with it like you did this morning so you can teach me how." *Okay, that sounded really inappropriate.*

"Uh, right. Where's your shirt?" Quinn braked to a stop and placed his feet to the ground.

"Right here," Blake said, shaking it from the waistband of his shorts. "It's hot out. Where's yours?"

"Spilled a latte on myself tonight and it stinks like hot, rotten milk now. I wrapped it in a ziplock bag and tossed it into my backpack."

"Oh." Blake jerked his thumb toward the dugout. "Go hide your bike back there next to mine."

"Okay, be right back."

When Quinn returned, Blake had rearranged the water jugs into a line and was thinking about making the water rise up from the jugs. Unfortunately, nothing happened. Quinn sat down on the other side of the water jugs.

"Ok, so, two questions: First, did you do something with water today, and second, did anything else weird happen?"

"Yes and yes. At work, when I was washing dishes, I was able to bend the stream of water from the faucet. I had to be careful because I didn't want anyone to see me."

"Okay, good. And you're right, whatever this is, we don't want anyone to know about it. Tell me what other weird thing happened today."

"Well, I um…I was—"

"Out with it," Blake said. "We're best friends and we're the only two people on the planet who can talk about this stuff, so no judgement."

"I was daydreaming about Keegan in physics when a couple of beakers shattered at the back of the room."

"Okay, that's weird. Was anyone mucking around back there?"

"Nope."

"And you weren't near them?"

"Well, I was in the middle of the room in my seat, but definitely not close enough to touch them."

"What happened in your daydream?" Blake didn't see Quinn blush in the night air.

"I kissed Keegan."

"Weird. A dream kiss makes glass explode."

"What about you?"

"Just the scorched earth thing after running and sweating my balls off. I finally cooled off, I think, but I still feel unusually warm."

Quinn looked around. "Probably one of the last hot nights of the summer. Nice to be outside to enjoy it."

"So, can you move the water?" Blake pointed to the line of jugs.

Quinn looked at the gallon in front of him and shrugged. "I don't know. Usually the water is already flowing, but I'll try."

Blake watched Quinn stare at the jug closest to him. It started vibrating on the ground.

Quinn smiled. "Yup, I can."

"Oh wow," Blake said, watching a ball of water rise up from the mouth of the jug. "Do something else with it."

"Like this?" Quinn asked. He raised his hand and flicked his fingers at Blake. The small ball of hovering water flew over the other two jugs and splashed Blake in the chest.

"Hey!" Blake exclaimed, laughing and looking at the water dripping down his torso. "That's amazing! How did you do that?"

"I'm honestly not sure. I think about what I want the water to do, and it happens, but it's not like I understand why it's happening."

"Do it again."

Quinn smiled at Blake and didn't break eye contact. Blake's mouth dropped open when he saw round orbs of water rise and levitate above the mouths of all three gallons of water. Then, he pointed at Quinn, whose eyes suddenly glowed bright blue.

"Tell me what you're doing," Blake whispered, mesmerized by the floating orbs of water that reflected the bright blue light coming from Quinn's eyes.

"I'm thinking about making the water float upward into a sphere. The only difference from now and this morning is that I don't feel what I felt in the shower—emotionally."

"What did you feel?"

"I don't remember, to be honest. I was in the shower thinking about how we lost the past couple of days. Try that, maybe?"

"Okay." Blake thought about being stuck in the hospital and became annoyed. "Don't get freaked out or anything, but your eyes are glowing blue."

Quinn put his hand up and saw the reflection of light on his palm. "I thought so. When your eyes glowed orange, you said you felt something behind your eyes; now, I do too. I can also see the blue reflecting on the water orbs."

"I wanna try. Don't help me."

"I'm not, but I can feel heat coming from your direction, like I'm sitting in front of a bonfire. Also, your eyes are glowing orange. Shit, the grass is on fire."

"What?" Blake exclaimed. He looked down. In the dark, it was easy to see a burning ring of grass expand outward from where he was sitting.

"Shit! Um, Water Boy, put it out!"

Quinn flicked his hand, and the floating water sprayed onto the grass, causing steam. "You are so *not* calling me Water Boy!" Quinn teased.

Blake laughed as the boys jumped up and each grabbed a gallon of water. They poured water around the edge of the six-foot-in-diameter circle of burnt grass, similar to the ones Blake had made in the parking lot.

"Coach is gonna be pissed at this," Quinn said, shaking his head.

"They won't know how to explain it. Now you know why I took my shirt off. I'm running hot," Blake explained. "Ever since yesterday."

"Maybe you're, like, Pyro, and I'm Iceman."

Blake rolled his eyes and stifled a small laugh. "First of all, Iceman makes ice. You can play with water, so that makes you Percy Jackson. That still doesn't explain the fact that we can sense each other or that you might have shattered glass in science class."

"Yeah, that sensing thing is kind of annoying. Is it going to happen all the time?"

Blake shrugged and sat down on unburnt grass.

Quinn sat next to him. "I bet it's permanent or will last until the effect of whatever happened fades away. Gosh, I hope it's not permanent."

"You don't? You were all excited about this superpower stuff less than twenty-four hours ago."

"I know," Quinn said, laying back on the grass and extending his arms out to his sides. "Now that it's really happening, I just think it's weird."

"Now you sound like me. What happened to Batman and Robin?"

"First of all, they don't have superpowers. Second, I just…it's really hard to hide superpowers from your parents. I mean, come on, glowing eyes? Peter Parker can barely do it with Aunt Mae and the girls he dates. A lot of the X-Men get taken away as kids because their parents can't handle it."

"Stop," Blake said, grabbing his best friend's hand. "You know why that happens? Because comics aren't real. Reality is so much more…" *What's the word I want?*

"Complicated?" Quinn suggested. "You're arguing yourself into a box."

"Whatever. I just mean, it's not as bad as you're making it out to be."

Quinn sat up and reached out with his hand. The gallon jug levitated two feet off the ground. "I don't know," he said.

Blake propped himself up to watch Quinn manipulate the water. The jug began descending toward the ground, but the water exited via the opening at the top, mimicked the shape of the jug, and hovered in the air. When the water had emptied, the jug dropped to the ground.

"That's amazing," Blake whispered.

Quinn stood up, his hand still extended toward the water.

"Stop the water from splashing all over you," Quinn said.

Blake jumped up. "Don't you dare!"

"Five seconds," Quinn challenged. "Stop the water."

Blake started laughing and jogged backward into the outfield. "No, don't, I can't."

"Three seconds."

"Quinn! Don't you dare!" Blake said, laughing.

Quinn started running after Blake. The water moved with him toward Blake.

"Oh shit," Blake said, turning to sprint away, but there was nothing to hide behind.

"One second."

"No!" Blake yelled, laughing hysterically.

Splash!

He cried out as a gallon of cool water exploded on his head and back. He turned around and charged at Quinn, who had doubled over in laughter. When Quinn looked up and saw Blake running at him, he put up his hands and yelled in mock surprise. Blake tackled him to the ground, and the boys wrestled around for a minute. Quinn, who had a fit of the giggles and couldn't defend himself against Blake's tickle attacks, quickly submitted and ended up on his back, pinned to the ground beneath Blake.

Breathing heavily, Quinn looked up at him and smiled. Blake met Quinn's gaze and smiled back, understanding the deep bond of friendship he shared with his best friend.

"It's really nice to see you smile, Blake," Quinn said.

Crash!

The boys looked toward the dugout where the noise had come from.

"Shit, the bikes," Blake whispered. Then he pushed himself up and charged full speed to the dugout. In a flash, Quinn was right behind him.

Blake grabbed the side of the dugout and used his momentum to swing around the corner. "Hey!" He crouched down and yelled out, hoping to scare any would-be thieves while hoping he wasn't surprising a skunk or raccoon.

No one was there, but the two bikes were lying on their sides.

Quinn came up behind him and braced his hands on his back and shoulder. "Anyone there?" he whispered.

Blake shook his head. "Not a soul."

"Think it's a new power?"

"Knocking over bikes?" Blake said, standing up.

Quinn nodded and pulled his hands off Blake. "Yeah, from the outfield, buddy."

He has a point. But which one of us did it?

Chapter 10
Life and Death

Quinn

Quinn rolled onto his back, a familiar urge beckoning him from deep within. He slid his hand across his stomach and under the waistband of his boxer shorts. He pushed the covers aside with his other hand.

Oh, Keegan.

Moments later his breath quickened and his chest heaved. Quinn inhaled sharply as euphoria spread through his body. Then, he felt power surge behind his eyes and assumed they were glowing blue.

On his desk, the glass of his banker's lamp cracked with a sharp sound. A picture frame jumped off the wall and fell to the floor, cracking the glass. Several DVDs jumped off his bookshelf and clattered to the floor, and the idle ceiling fan above him wiggled in place. He peeled open an eye in horror and saw several books slide off his shelf and drop to the floor with several thuds. Then his dresser shook in place, knocking over all the picture frames and random stuff he had set on top of it. His desk chair rolled several inches to the right of where it had rested all night.

What the hell? Did we have an earthquake? Or was that me?

The unusually loud thudding of footsteps climbing the stairs alerted him to one of his dad's imminent presence.

Eek! He can't see me like this. And why do those footsteps seem so loud to me?

He raised his butt and pulled his boxers up a little higher to cover his fading arousal and most of the mess. Then, he covered himself with the blankets, holding his hand over his abdomen.

My eyes! Stop glowing. Calm thoughts, calm thoughts!

The footsteps approached his door and stopped. His eyes jumped up from the threshold to the knocking sound at the center of the door. Somehow, he knew exactly where his dad's knuckles rapped on the wooden door. He winced at the loudness of the knocking.

"Quinn? Are you all right?" Dad asked.

Quinn opened his mouth and covered his ears. His dad may as well have been shouting in his ears. "Yeah, I'm okay, Dad, I just, uh, dropped some books."

"Do you need help?" *Why is he so damn loud? This hurts!*

"No, nope, I'm good. I can pick up my books."

"You're sure?"

"I just, uh, I need a minute, Dad." Quinn shook his head, trying to focus on balancing out the sound. He turned his head at a clicking sound. In the corner of the room above the door, near the ceiling, he saw—with incredible clarity—a small spider weaving a web. *What the heck?*

"Okay. Um, by the way, you're supposed to be at work in thirty minutes."

"Oh crap!" Quinn exclaimed, wincing again at the loudness of his voice.

He threw the covers off and jumped out of bed. He paused, no longer feeling the power behind his eyes. *Thank goodness.*

He grabbed his towel from behind the door, then pulled open the door, doing the best he could to hide the evidence. He nearly ran into Dad, who caught him by the shoulders.

"Hey," Dad practically shouted, looking at Quinn's pained face. "You okay, son?"

Too loud, please stop talking, please… This is way too awkward.

"I'm fine, really, I just…" *Please don't start checking me over. I'm not injured. You don't need to see…*

"Oh!" Dad said, his eyes opening wide. He let go of Quinn's shoulders and stepped back. "Right, gotcha. Um, let me know if you want a ride."

"That would be great!" Quinn said, dashing past his father into the bathroom. He closed the door behind him and took a deep breath. It slammed and echoed louder than it should have in his ears.

Great, he totally knows what I was doing in there.

In New England, the Saturday after Labor Day weekend should be less busy than the holiday weekend, but in Portsmouth, that's never the case. From the moment Quinn clocked in at Breaking New Grounds, he didn't stop working. Outside on the large sidewalk patio, tourists and locals enjoyed varieties of tea, coffee, and baked goods as they reveled in the unseasonably warm weather.

Quinn finished cashing out a customer and headed to the front of the counter to serve the next customer. His eyes locked with Keegan's.

"Can I help you?" Cassie asked Keegan.

Dammit. She beat me to him. Shit, no eyes, no eyes, no glowing eyes.

As he passed behind Cassie he nodded at Keegan, who winked back at him.

Why does he have to be so adorable all the time? No exploding things...please...

Then Keegan placed his order with Cassie.

"Can I help you?" Quinn asked a man in his thirties, shifting his eyes to Keegan whenever possible. The fear of superpowered happenings did little to stifle Quinn's attraction to Keegan. Even standing in line, he was mesmerized by Keegan's beautiful face, his stunning blue eyes, and his cute messy-styled hair that poked out from beneath a Clippers baseball cap that day.

He took the thirty-something's order for a large green tea with lemon to go and brought it to the register, but he had to wait for Max to finish cashing out a frazzled mother and her adorable but hyper-excited toddler. He tried to act natural and catch Keegan's eyes, but his crush was lost in his phone, furiously typing away while grinning from ear to ear.

Quinn turned his back to Keegan and grabbed a large to-go cup. He dropped in the green tea bags and added hot water, glancing back at Keegan, who was still focused on his phone.

He felt himself become aggravated with Keegan's distraction and decided to try and talk with him once he cashed out the thirty-something. Instead, heat near his hand distracted him. He looked down at the water in the paper cup and saw it was rapidly boiling.

What the hell?

His hand moved quickly and he set the cup on the counter edge. The moment he let go, the water stopped boiling.

Oh cool, I can make things hot, too! At least nothing shattered this time.

Then, Quinn panicked.

Oh crap! Please, don't burn down the coffee shop or scorch the floor.

Quinn looked at the floor around him. Thankfully, it hadn't scorched…yet.

Just calm down. These things don't seem to happen when you're calm. Breathe.

When he felt relaxed, he dumped the tea into the sink and tossed the cup into the trash. Then he looked at the thirty-something guy, who watched him with intense curiosity.

"Uh, sorry," Quinn said. "There was a…hornet in the cup…I didn't see it earlier."

The man's eyes widened and he nodded. "Thanks for catching that."

Quinn remade the green tea, and this time the water didn't boil. When he handed over the tea and returned the man's change, he looked around for Keegan.

Quinn's shoulders dropped. Keegan was already heading out of the shop with his beverage.

If you don't try to say hi to him, you'll lose your chance. Talking to him here is way better than at school.

"I'll be right back," Quinn called out to Matt, his manager.

"Uh, okay?" Matt answered. "We're really busy, make it quick."

In a flash, Quinn dashed to the backside of the coffee shop and jogged around some unpacked boxes to the employee and delivery entrance. For a moment, the usually busy Daniel Street was quiet. Quinn looked left and right for Keegan but didn't see him.

He must be in the public square out front.

Quinn turned left to run to the square but stopped, thinking his mind had played a trick on him. He turned around and looked up Daniel Street again, remembering how clearly he had seen the spider in his bedroom. An expensive red car with a throaty engine was speeding toward the stop sign at the square behind him. Between him and the car, the frazzled mother and her young son were crossing the street, except the toddler had dropped his bouncy ball and had wrenched his hand free to chase after it—directly into the path of the oblivious speed demon.

The mother screamed and stepped forward, but when the oncoming car didn't slow down, she hesitated. People turned their heads and gasped as the horrific finality of the impending accident flashed in their minds.

"My baby!" she cried out, deciding to try and save her son as the seconds ticked. Quinn looked—with his newfound enhanced vision—at the driver of the car and clearly saw he was distracted, either texting on his phone or tinkering with the car's radio.

Oh my gosh, they're both going to die!

"No!" Quinn shouted at the last second. He closed his eyes, feeling the power surge behind them. He didn't want anyone to see them glow blue and he didn't want to watch the mother or her son splatter over the hood of the car.

Bang!

Pop!

Screams!

Crunch!

Slam!

Silence.

"Oh, thank goodness!" a man exclaimed.

What?

Quinn opened his eyes, shielding them from onlookers, as the joyful sobbing of a mother and the confused crying of a startled toddler reached his ears.

"What happened to the car?" another woman asked.

Quinn looked at the car. *Oh no.*

The entire front was smashed in like it had struck an invisible cement wall. The hood was folded like an accordion, and Quinn's enhanced vision showed him the detail of every crack in the shattered windshield. He noticed the airbags had deployed as the crumpled driver door creaked opened and a man staggered out, clutching his phone with one hand.

"You're a real jerk," a woman shouted, "texting and driving like that. You could have killed that little boy."

Quinn leaned against the cool brick, stunned at what he had seen. He felt the blood drain from his head, and he blinked his eyes to focus. Thankfully, they had powered down.

I think I just stopped that car.

A police cruiser turned right onto Daniel Street from Chapel Street and pulled up, its blue lights flashing. People stepped out of the local businesses to gawk. Quinn touched his head, shock dulling the powerful sense of proximity to Blake. He had stepped out of Kaffee VonSolln to gawk, but now, Quinn knew, Blake walked toward him. Quinn stepped forward and looked around the bank sign and caught Blake's eye. His friend waved at him and started jogging toward him, and Quinn took a few shaky steps but slumped to the ground, unable to stand up.

Blake picked up his pace and approached. "Hey, Quinn, are you all right?" Blake asked, squatting near him.

Quinn shook his head and took a deep breath. "No." His voice wavered and his hands began shaking.

"Hey, buddy, it's okay, I've got you," Blake said, sitting down and wrapping his left arm around Quinn's shoulders. "The kid didn't get hit. I don't know how, but—" Blake paused. "Wait, did you...?" His mouth dropped open and his eyes opened wide.

"I could have killed that driver," Quinn whispered.

"You stopped the car, didn't you?"

"I don't know," Quinn said, still shaking.

"Tell me what you did, Quinn. How did you stop it?"

Quinn shrugged. "I saw him texting or something; he wasn't looking at the road. I just closed my eyes because I didn't want to see the kid get hit and shouted, '*No.*' Then I heard the car slam into...thin air."

"You saved that kid's life, and probably his mother's as well."

"But I almost killed that driver. I don't want this thing anymore. I want it gone. It's too much. I made water boil in my hands earlier when Keegan came into the shop and now I almost killed someone. I want a normal junior year and I want to go to UNH in two years…but this thing, I can't, I just can't."

"Hey, slow down, buddy. One day at a time."

"You don't get it," Quinn said. "Things aren't happening as fast for you. When I least expect it, something unexpected happens. Today my hearing and vision are like, on overdrive, and I almost burned the damn coffee shop down and I stopped a speeding car *with my mind*. I can't do this!"

Quinn buried his head in his hands and broke down. Blake pulled him in, allowing Quinn to lean into his chest and weep for several minutes.

"So, you saw Keegan today, huh?" Blake said. Quinn noted the soft tone in his voice; he was trying to distract him from the crisis.

Quinn chuckled and sniffled. "Yeah, he's the entire reason I was out here. I tried to serve him, but Cassie beat me to it. I figured I'd run out and try to say hi, but this happened. That mother and her kid were in the shop a few minutes ago."

"If you hadn't tried to catch up with Keegan, that kid wouldn't be alive right now and his mother would be on her way to the hospital and the news reports would be horrible."

"But I—"

"It doesn't matter what you almost did. The driver is walking after you did whatever you did. That's the most important part. As for his wrecked car, he deserved that for doing something as stupid as texting and driving."

"I guess so," Quinn said with a shrug.

"I know so."

"All right, all right. Shit, I gotta get back inside. Matt's gonna kill me."

"Sure, but first, I wish someone had a camera."

"Why's that?" Quinn asked,

"Think about it. This is an ironic, picturesque moment," Blake responded. "A VonSolln guy is consoling a BNG guy."

Quinn rolled his eyes and laughed as the boys stood up.

"You okay?" Blake asked, looking into his eyes.

"Yeah," Quinn said, returning the tender gaze. "Thanks."

Blake winked at him. "Talk to you later."

"For sure."

Quinn hung his bike in the garage on the wall hooks and tapped the white garage door button on his way into the house. The garage door rumbled shut behind him as he made his way into the house, the sound fading when the inside door shut. He kicked off his coffee-stained work shoes and set them on the mud mat before making his way down the hall to the kitchen.

"Hey," Dad said, washing dishes at the counter. He shot Quinn a quick glance. "Dinner's almost ready. We're grilling veggies and steak tips tonight. Well, Daddio is, not me. My job, of course, is cleaning the dishes and making sure the jasmine rice simmers nicely without boiling over."

Quinn chuckled. "Sounds good, I'm starved." The last time Dad tried to grill steak tips, he'd burned them, and the trio had ordered pizza instead.

"Hey, kiddo," Daddio said, walking in from the outside where the deck and barbecue grill were kept. He walked over to Quinn and hugged him, gently kissing him on the head. "You stink like coffee," he teased.

"Yeah, I need a quick shower. Do I have time?"

Daddio checked his watch. "You have nineteen minutes. The tips just went on the grill."

"Oh hey," Dad said, gesturing like he was remembering something. "There was an accident on Daniel Street today. Did you see it at all?"

"Yeah," Quinn said, unable to hide his sorrow at the event. He froze in place and swallowed hard. *What do I say?*

"You okay?" Dad asked, stepping away from the sink. Daddio put his arm around Quinn's shoulders.

"I was standing outside when it happened…I almost saw a toddler get creamed by an asshole in a sports car who wasn't paying attention."

"Oh my gosh," Daddio said, squeezing Quinn's shoulders. "That's horrible!"

"Oh, Quinn," Dad said, "I'm sorry you had to see that."

"Almost see it," Quinn said, correcting his father.

"The news said the car was smashed and no one was hurt, except for some airbag burns and bruises for the driver."

Quinn nodded.

"How did the car get smashed up?"

How am I going to explain my way out of this one? Oh, I know!

"Well," Quinn said, looking at the floor. "My timing was a bit off. I wasn't outside when it happened, I was in the stock room unpacking a shipment. When I heard a car hit something, I poked my head out the side door to see what was going on. That's when I saw a woman who had just been at the register grabbing her kid from the street. I don't know what the car hit, but it was pretty smashed up. The driver got out and was walking around, so I guess that's good."

"Absolutely. It's great no one got hurt today," Dad said.

"Still, that little kid was probably three years old. Maybe four. He almost died."

"But he didn't, and neither did the driver, right?" Daddio asked.

Quinn shrugged. "I know you're right, it's still shocking to me, that's all."

Daddio's watch beeped, startling them all. "Sorry to ruin the moment, but I gotta go rotate the steak tips."

Quinn chuckled. "Please do, the last thing we want is burnt steak, right?" he asked, gently teasing his other father.

Dad rolled his eyes and smiled. "Sure, pick on the guy who can barely boil water. I get it."

"Love ya, kiddo," Daddio said, giving him another kiss. "Now go shower and rinse the super-stink of work off you. You got less than fifteen minutes, okay? And Quinn?" Daddio said, heading toward the door.

"Yeah?"

"Thanks for talking with us."

Quinn smiled. "Sure thing."

Then he headed upstairs to shower.

Quinn flipped through an old Superman comic book and tried to focus on the words, but they remained elusive to his distracted mind.

Am I ever going to understand how this thing works? What happens when I have a choice to use my powers for good and I don't because I'm afraid? Will that make me a bad person?

"Hey, Quinn?" Daddio called out, standing in the hallway on the other side of his cracked-open bedroom door.

Surprised, Quinn jumped halfway across the bed.

"Oh, hey, sorry, son, didn't mean to scare you."

Something odd caught his eye in the dresser mirror. Rather, something didn't catch his eye—his reflection. *Oh crap, am I invisible?*

"Are you okay?"

The door started to push open, and Quinn rolled off the bed and onto the floor on the far side of the bed, opposite the bedroom door. He pulled off his tank top as fast as he could and started to do push-ups.

Oh shit, come on, go back to normal!

"Yup," he called out, exaggerating his labor.

The door creaked open more. "Am I bothering you?"

"Nope!" he exclaimed.

"Where are you? What are you doing?"

Please, please go back to normal.

Quinn popped up and ran a hand through his hair. Daddio locked eyes with him and smiled. "You're working out?"

"Yeah, just had some frustrations to burn, so I'm doing some push-ups." *I guess I'm not invisible anymore.*

"Ah. We're gonna grab some ice cream downtown, did you want to come with?"

"Yeah," he said, reaching for his tank top.

Daddio sat down on the edge of his bed.

Uh oh.

"You're sure you're all right?"

"Yeah, why?" Quinn said, pulling on his shirt and standing up.

Daddio's brow wrinkled. "You're just…off tonight. That accident today, almost seeing a child die—"

"Yeah, it's messed me up a little."

"Okay, fair enough. You know you can talk to us about that, right?"

"Of course, Daddio," Quinn said, running a hand through his hair again.

"Or anything else you want to talk about. We love you for who you are, no matter what."

"Yeah," Quinn said, his face scrunching with confusion.

"Like, anything else, Quinn," Daddio repeated.

"Did you have something in mind?"

"Yeah. Dad told me about this morning. You *know* we don't care about that, right?"

Quinn's eyes bulged open. "Oh, right. That. Yeah, I know. Thanks."

"Okay then." Daddio pushed himself up from the bed. "Well, shall we? Ice cream awaits."

"Annabelle's or Izzy's?" Quinn asked, following his father out the door.

"Tough call," Daddio chuckled. "Thumb wrestle you for it?"

"Sure thing. But Dad has to judge it because you cheat," Quinn teased.

Daddio clutched his chest and dropped his mouth open with surprise. "I do not!"

"Uh-huh, whatever, Daddio," Quinn said. The two laughed as they made their way downstairs to get Dad from the living room and head out for ice cream.

Chapter 11

No Thank You

Blake

The early morning coffee shift never appealed to Blake, especially on weekends when all he wanted to do was sleep in till ten o'clock or later. He couldn't understand how or why people got up so early on weekends, except the retired folk. They tended to get up early no matter what, along with a bunch of folks who were crazy enough to run or exercise at one of the local gyms first thing in the morning—and most of them needed their coffee fix.

Still, he couldn't complain—Quinn always had to be up earlier because BNG opened at six thirty. Kaffee VonSolln opened at eight o'clock, but the morning baristas need to be at the shop at least thirty minutes prior to opening to set up. That didn't stop the diehards from lining up for their coffee.

Today, though, he did not mind getting up early and getting out of the house. Last night, his parents had gone to one of the local legion bars, and his father had imbibed far too many drinks and barely made it home. Other patrons had to help put his drunken father into the car so his mother could unsafely drive them home. When she'd gotten home, she'd woken Blake up and asked him to help bring his father inside because he had passed out. Blake had carried his unconscious father into the house, where he'd dropped him into his favorite recliner. His mother had apologized profusely, but Blake had shrugged it off, telling her it didn't matter because she enabled him.

As he pedaled to work, his mind drifted away from his drunken father back to his late-night texts with Quinn, who still struggled with the mystery of their developing superpowers. Blake felt envious of his buddy's more obvious and seemingly easier powers but kept his mouth shut.

If I had those powers, I'd fix Darien for good and make sure bullies like him stop picking on the little guys. Who knows, maybe it would be cool to be closet superheroes. Or, better yet, what could I gain by taking things from others? Quinn's had it easy, but I've had to scrape along and find my way. It isn't fair. Maybe it's time I exploit others to get ahead the way they've exploited me.

Blake absentmindedly aimed his bike for a puddle and sighed.

If only I could figure out—

Ka-thunk!

The front tire of Blake's bike dropped down into the puddle and abruptly stopped spinning. The back wheel came off the ground and proceeded to rotate upward over the front axle, causing Blake to endo, or flip over the handlebars and crash.

Shit!

Blake saw the ground coming at him, and he closed his eyes and placed his hands in front of him.

This is gonna hurt.

But there was no pain. Blake peeled open an eye and saw the ground several inches beneath his body.

What the heck? Am I floating?

A split second later, Blake's body dropped to the ground and he grunted. "Oh man," Blake said. Then he realized he'd spoken out loud. He looked around, but there were no signs of life around him and he didn't think anyone had heard his bike crash to the pavement. He pushed himself off the ground and picked up his bike. Since he hadn't hit the ground, he wasn't sore or in pain. He checked the front tire, which miraculously had not punctured. The wheel's rim and spokes didn't seem damaged, but his front wheel-to-handlebar alignment was off a few degrees.

He pulled out his phone and texted Quinn: Need to talk to you after work - something new.

He pocketed his phone and looked around again. He still didn't see anyone. He shrugged, mounted his bike, and pedaled to the shop.

Blake pedaled through Strawberry Banke to Prescott Park. He crossed the grassy park and scanned the three public piers for Quinn, spotting him and his bike on the pier closest to the Memorial Bridge. He shook his head when the overwhelming sense of proximity to Quinn echoed in his mind. The sensing thing seemed easier to handle today.

The Piscataqua River rushed beneath his feet as he walked his bike to the lookout where Quinn, shirtless, was getting some sun while watching the Moran tugboats guide a large cargo ship to the waterway under the raised drawbridge. Quinn glanced over his shoulder when he heard Blake approaching.

"Hey, what's up? *Sensed* you coming," Quinn teased.

"Yeah, that's not going away, is it?"

"Nope, I don't think so."

"I have something important to tell you," Blake said, resting his bike against the wooden railings. He pulled off his coffee-smelling T-shirt and tucked it into his jeans. Then he leaned on the railing next to Quinn and watched the ship as it passed under the bridge.

"You okay?" Blake asked, noting the odd quiet surrounding his buddy.

Quinn nodded. "Yeah, didn't sleep well, and it was crazy busy today."

"You gonna be able to go running in a bit?" Blake asked. Coach expected them to run seven miles that day.

"Yeah, I'll be fine. So, what's this news?"

"I flew today," Blake said softly.

Quinn spun around and stared at Blake. "You're kidding."

"Well, more like levitated or floated...I'm not really sure which." Blake shared his spectacular morning wipeout with Quinn and described the sensation of hovering over the ground for a few seconds. The boys leaned over the railing again and stared at the churning river water.

"Saw my life flash before my eyes when I endo'd. Bottom line, my face should be torn up with road rash, but it's not."

"Wow," Quinn said. "That would be the best superpower ever."

"Flight?"

"Yeah."

"I dunno. I think I'd rather be able to move things like Magneto can, but move anything—not just metals."

"I stand corrected. I'd rather do that than fly."

"What are you two lovebirds up to?" a harsh, familiar voice called out.

Quinn's shoulders dropped in disappointment as he glanced over his shoulder.

"Great, just who I wanted to bump into today," Blake muttered, his soul descending into anger and frustration.

"Careful, Blake," Quinn whispered. "We don't need to set off any of our known or unknown powers in public. Still, it'd be fun to soak him with dirty harbor water. That I could do right now."

Blake chuckled.

Darien's flip-flops smacked the wooden decking as he approached. He was alone; Kyle and Tony were nowhere to be seen.

Not today.

Blake turned around and stepped forward. "You can turn around and get lost, Darien. We are not in the mood for your bullshit today."

Darien stopped, his face awash with astonishment. "Okay, okay. Sheesh, I only wanted to say hi to my best friends."

"We're not your best friends, Darien," Blake said. "Best friends don't harass and bully each other the way you do."

"You're right," Darien said, offering a smile that quickly turned wicked. "What was I thinking? You guys suck. See you later, losers." Darien flipped them the bird and turned. He retraced his footsteps across Prescott Park and retreated.

Quinn shook his head and leaned on the railing again. "He's not as big an asshole when he doesn't have an audience."

Blake chuckled and rested his hands on the railing in front of him. The aft section of the cargo ship and the last tugboat passed under the drawbridge. "So you're really certain that's what this is, we have superpowers?" Blake asked. "I know we've said it jokingly, but—"

Quinn nodded. "Totally. I think we're gaining superpowers. How else do you explain what's going on? The only thing I can't figure out is how or why they get triggered when they do."

"I know what you mean. But you seem to control yours, right? I mean, like the water thing you can do."

Quinn shrugged. "That's where it falls apart. I wasn't angry or falling off my bicycle. I was showering when it started. You get upset with Darien and burn the ground. I boiled water with a customer near me. How this is all happening doesn't make any sense to me, and it's frustrating as hell, especially when somehow I stopped that car and—"

Quinn stopped and stared at the drawbridge as it slowly descended to road-level height so traffic between Maine and New Hampshire could resume.

"Saved that kid's life?"

"Yeah," Quinn said softly.

"I know that upsets you, but you did a good thing."

"But what if we never figure this out, Blake? What if we're just one big, hidden danger to our families and friends? Hell, what if we blow up the school or something? What if our chances for a normal life were destroyed in that stupid cave?"

"All right, stop," Blake said. "Take a deep breath. Seriously!"

Quinn side-eyed Blake.

"I mean it, take a deep breath."

Quinn inhaled and exhaled.

"You're *Mister Positivity* around here. You're the one who's always helping people, pulling them up when they're down, and encouraging them when they feel like failures. What would you be telling yourself right now?"

Quinn chuckled. "I have no idea, dude. That's why I'm freaking out."

"Okay, try it a different way. We've loved comic books and superhero things since we were kids, when we've always wanted superpowers. Now, we have a strong possibility of having what no one else has. What have you always said you'd do with superpowers?"

Quinn chuckled. "That I'd use my powers to help people and do good things, just like a real superhero would."

"All right, then. That's what you'll do."

"What about you?"

"I will not be your sidekick," Blake said, chuckling.

"What about becoming a dynamic duo with an equal partnership?" Quinn asked.

"Maybe. But honestly, I don't want to do the same things you do. I want to figure out how to put people like Darien in their place."

"That doesn't sound like being a superhero," Quinn said hesitantly.

"Oh, it is, just in a different way. Sometimes the bullies need to get cut."

"Are you talking about hurting people?"

"Not badly."

Quinn rolled his eyes. "You just can't become the super villain, okay? The last thing I need is to fight my best friend."

"Right."

Bells rang out as the red and white crossing gates on the bridge raised so cars could traverse over the bridge once more.

"I really think we need to talk with Mr. St. Germain tomorrow after school or during his free period."

"You're sure about that?" Blake asked, swatting a fly away.

"Yeah, we need to talk with someone about this, and he knows so much geeky stuff about comic book superheroes. He'd be perfect, and I trust him. I bet he could help us figure out how to control what's going on with these powers. I'm pretty sure, given how much he loves comics, he'd be totally cool knowing and protecting our secret identities and all that. If we can get him in the science room with the lab stations, I have just the trick to prove to him that we're not crazy."

"Well, that didn't take long," Blake said, smiling.

"What do you mean?"

"Five minutes ago, you were all upset about having these powers, now you're all about learning how to use them and building a team."

Quinn smiled. "Hey, talking to you helped. If we could control them, we won't be so scary or dangerous to people. You know what happens if the police—or people like Victor Kraze—catch on to our level of freak. We get captured and experimented on by the government."

Blake burst out laughing. "We definitely watch too much TV."

Blake sat cross-legged on his bed in his red boxer shorts, staring at the cup of water across the room on his desk. He tried to make the water float, splash, bubble, move, anything that Quinn could do with water.

Nothing.

Downstairs, his parents argued with loud voices about his dad's lack of consideration toward his mom and Blake. He struggled to tune it out because now, like Quinn, his hearing and vision had become enhanced, and he struggled to control them. For the past hour, kitchen cabinets had slammed and hands had pounded on countertops or the kitchen table—all excruciatingly painful sounds to Blake.

Blake rolled his eyes and shook his head when his father started swearing at his mother. He'd probably head out to one of the local bars and drink away his anger and problems until they kicked him out—if the bouncers even let him in—while his mom sat at home crying to herself while watching reality television.

"Blake!" his father, Ralph, yelled. "Get down here!"

Startled, Blake froze at his father's incredibly loud voice. He blinked his eyes and shook his head to alleviate the pain. He took a deep breath, uncrossed his legs, and pushed himself up. Then he padded down the stairs in his bare feet and walked into the kitchen.

"Yeah?" he said with more annoyance than he wanted to.

"It's not his fault," Stella, his mother, said, in tears.

"This is totally his fault," Ralph ranted, shoving a folded letter at him.

Blake noted their voices came through at normal volume while they were in the same room. Blake's brow wrinkled as he reached for the paper, his father shaking it impatiently. He took it from his father and unfolded it. "What's this?" he asked, trying to make sense of the strange-looking letter.

"This," Ralph said, grabbing the paper out of Blake's hand and shaking it, "is your fucking hospital bill." He shoved the letter back into Blake's hand and pointed—slapped—the bottom of the letter where some larger print announced: Amount Due: $29,568.00.

Blake's heart sank. Under it, smaller print indicated the hospital would try to bill their insurance first, but he knew their meager insurance would be insufficient to cover that kind of damage.

"I should sue Quinn's parents for this. If you hadn't gone with them—"

"It's not their fault," Blake said, trying to keep his temper calm. The last thing he wanted to do was scorch the kitchen or set fire to his house.

"Don't talk back to me," his father yelled, stepping closer to Blake.

Blake looked up from the letter, surprised. His father rarely threatened him with physical violence. *Is this gonna be one of those times?*

"I'm just saying that—"

"You're saying nothing!" Ralph snapped. "The hospital is gouging us for thirty thousand dollars because you passed out in the woods and had to stay there four nights, not to mention a stupidly expensive ambulance ride."

Blake stared at his father, unable to speak.

"He did die, Ralph," Stella argued, her voice wavering as she recalled the circumstances of the accident. "They were struck by lightning and died when they got to the hospital, then they had to resuscitate him. Then they kept him for observation. You don't think that wasn't cheap?"

Ralph turned around and stared at his wife. "Whose side are you on, Stella? Ours or theirs?"

"Ours, of course," Stella snapped.

"Then stop defending them."

"What do you want me to do?" Blake inquired, not wanting to participate in a useless fight that wouldn't make anything better. "I don't make enough money at the coffee shop to pay that back, and Quinn—"

"Quinn," Ralph echoed loudly. "I ought to forbid you from seeing that queer boy. He's nothing but trouble, and look at the mess he's gotten us into."

The words against Quinn stung bitterly. The light bulbs flickered briefly and made a strange zapping sound. At the same time, Blake noticed sweat beading on his father's forehead as his mother fanned herself.

Oh shit.

"That boy," Blake said angrily, feeling his temperature running hot, "is my best friend, and I'm not going to stop seeing him no matter what you say. It's not like we're twelve and we robbed a store. We had an accident on a camping trip!"

"And you're alive," Stella added.

"I need to go outside," Blake said, his voice trembling with rage and hurt. He sidestepped past his father, careful not to touch him, and made his way to the back door. A recessed light bulb flashed and popped in its fixture above him.

"I'm not done with you, get back here."

"I need to go outside," Blake repeated. "It's too hot in here." *I need to get out before I burn you alive.*

"Dammit," his father said, wiping his forehead. "Why is it so hot in here?" Then he followed his son out the door. "Hey, where do you think you're going?"

"I'm just going outside!" Blake yelled, reaching for the door knob and hesitating at the last second. *Please don't melt.*

He grabbed the metal knob and opened the door. It remained intact, but he felt the temperature difference between his hot hand and the room-temperature knob.

"Get back here," his father yelled, chasing after him.

"I don't feel well, I need to get outside," Blake insisted. "Leave me alone."

Blake looked around as he hustled across the small deck in his bare feet to the stairs that brought him down to the concrete patio. It was about ten feet across and twelve feet deep. *I hope this is big enough.*

He wrapped his arms around himself like he was cold and tried to calm down.

"I will not leave you alone!" Ralph said, standing on the top of the deck. "I don't make enough money to pay this. Neither does your mother."

"So what do you want me to do about it?" Blake yelled, exasperated, trying to figure out where to escape to since he couldn't stop the intense heat he felt across his shirtless body. "It's not my goddamn fault I got struck by lightning!"

"You're an idiot, Blake," Ralph snapped. "A stupid, motherfucking..."

Blake grimaced as the familiar words cut deep.

114

"lazy, good-for-nothing kid…"

Across the street, the street light sizzled and popped. The houselights around him blinked on and off as if the neighborhood was experiencing a brownout. *Wait, am I doing that?*

"who will never amount to anything big in this world."

Blake sensed electricity pulsing and flowing in the air around him.

"Take that back!" he yelled, dropping his hands in anger and stepping forward. Then he stopped, catching himself. *Aw, crap, too late.*

The outside lights of the nearby houses flashed, popped, and went out. Around him, Blake felt heat explode outward from his body. Power churned behind his eyes. *Shit, they're glowing. Don't look at Dad.*

He looked down and saw the concrete scorching around him. He briefly looked up to see his father distracted by the blinking and popping lights around them. In the dark, he wouldn't notice the burnt concrete.

Blake turned and ran past the house to the sidewalk, forgetting he only wore boxer shorts. He ran *fast* down the street to the house with the in-ground pool owned by the older couple he had mowed lawns for when he was thirteen to make extra cash. He knew it'd be risky and hoped his feet didn't leave burnt footprints on the sidewalk, but he needed to cool himself down somehow before he accidentally hurt his dad.

Running faster than usual, he approached the fenced yard of the large house. He saw lights in the front of the house and hoped no one was in the back. Somewhere behind him, his father was calling his name and cursing after him. He flipped the latch to the fence gate and let himself quietly into the backyard and then lowered himself into the shallow end of the pool. The cool September water steamed and hissed around him as it reacted to the high temperature of his skin.

Seriously? How hot am I?

He waded, then swam, to the deeper part of the pool and took a deep breath. Then he let himself sink under the cool water.

Peace.

Only the loud hum of the filter pump—enhanced by his new hearing power—and the gurgling noises of the skimmer reached his ears. When his lungs should have begged for air, he swam upward and quietly exhaled while looking around. No one was there. The water around his shoulders bubbled, and he could see the steam rising off his nose. He raised a hand out of the water and watched the steam disappear into the night sky. Several more deep breaths and journeys under the water's surface cooled him off, both physically and emotionally.

Finally, his eyes stopped glowing.

Blake swam back to the shallow end and quietly pushed himself out of the pool. He sat on the edge, his feet dangling in the water, not ready to leave the serenity he had discovered. He adjusted his cotton boxers and noted how they looked darker, but not from being wet—they looked as though they had been evenly burned. *Great, just great. One of these days I'm gonna burn my clothes off and find myself naked in front of someone.*

He sighed and closed his eyes momentarily to listen. His father was no longer calling for him. *Guess I'll have to deal with him one way or the other.*

Blake stood, trying not to make too many splashing or dripping sounds, and then made his way back to his house.

Chapter 12

Answers

Quinn

"Hey, Mr. St. Germain," Quinn said, greeting his science teacher as he walked into the empty science lab their teacher had dubbed the Lair of Awesomeness. Blake followed behind him.

Mr. St. Germain looked up from a book and smiled. "Hey, guys, what's up?"

"Can we talk to you?" Quinn asked nervously, his voice wavering. "In private?"

"Um, sure. Shut the door. That's about the best I can do for you in a classroom."

"Thanks," Blake said, closing the door.

Quinn purposely walked over to one of the black and faux-wood lab tables with running water and turned on the cold tap. Blake walked up next to him and stood on Quinn's left side.

"I think you'll want to come see this."

"Okay," Mr. St. Germain said, sighing as he tilted his head to one side. "You boys aren't pranking me, right?"

"Not at all," Quinn said, vigorously shaking his head from side to side.

Mr. St. Germain pushed himself up from his squeaky desk chair and walked through a row of student desks to the lab side of the classroom.

"We just need to make sure we can swear you to secrecy," Blake said.

"Um, well, I can't promise that. As a teacher, I'm an obligatory reporter. If you or someone you know plans on hurting themselves—"

Quinn waved his hand. "It's nothing like that, I promise," he said, interrupting his teacher. "This is just, uh, really sensitive information, and we can't trust just anyone with it. That's why we need you to swear to secrecy."

Mr. St. Germain stopped at the lab table and looked at the running water, then at Blake, then at Quinn. "Are you boys in trouble? And is there a reason you're running the cold water?"

"Yes. But first you have to promise not to tell anyone what we're about to show you."

"Maybe. No promises. No swearing of secrecy—yet."

Quinn looked at Blake, who shrugged at him. "We have no choice, Quinn. We picked him for a reason."

"Picked me?" Mr. St. Germain repeated.

Quinn nodded. *Here goes nothing.*

"Do you remember several weeks ago when you were talking about the X-Men's origin stories, and how some of them got their superpowers in strange, unexplainable ways? Like the Incredible Hulk through accidental exposure to gamma rays?"

"The Hulk is an Avenger, not one of the X-Men. Those are mutants who are born with unique abilities that emerge at some point in time, if not at birth. That's completely different from—"

"Yeah," Quinn said, raising his hand. "We get it. We're talking about non-mutants and non-aliens like Superman, but the ones who acquired their superpowers like the Hulk, the Flash, or the Green Lantern."

"Does Deadpool count?" Blake asked.

"Good question," Quinn answered.

"Maybe," Mr. St. Germain said, nodding to the sink. "And the water is running why?"

"When those folks got their superpowers, did they know what was going on at first?"

"Of course not," Mr. St. Germain said, smiling, ready to share a seed of truth from his wealth of comic knowledge. "There was a lot of trial and error before they figured out what was going on with them. Kinda like your bodies going through puberty. It can be obnoxious as heck, but it's totally necessary to learn and grow into young adults. All of those comic characters who acquired their powers had to learn what triggered their powers, how to temper or control their powers if they could, and how to use them for good or, if they were the villains, evil. For a lot of those folks, everything changed in one day, and they couldn't go back to their old life even if they wanted to, no matter how hard they tried."

"And who helped those folks?"

"Well," Mr. St. Germain said, crossing his arms while thinking for a moment. "Most of them had some kind of mentor to help them sort out their abilities and adapt to normal life while balancing their superhero lives with their everyday lives. That's not always the case, though. Spider-man didn't have a mentor, but that depends on which storyline you're following. You still haven't told me why the water is running. Do you think the room is bugged and you're trying to make white noise?"

Quinn looked at Blake and nodded. Blake walked around Quinn and positioned himself so his body blocked the view of the water faucet from the classroom door's window.

Quinn swallowed and looked his teacher in the eyes. "Well, Mr. St. Germain, it's no longer a comic book story, because that day came and went for us. Today, this is the day everything changes for you."

Mr. St. Germain's right eyebrow curled up. "Quinn, are you, um—"

"What?" Quinn said, eyeing Blake nervously.

"Are you trying to come out to me?"

Blake burst out laughing and clapped his hands together.

Holy crap, how did he miss all the hints we've been putting in front of him?

"It's totally okay, you know. I don't care if you're gay or straight in my classroom. I just want you to get a good grade."

"Yeah, um, that's not what we're talking about, at all," Quinn said.

"Oh. I'm sorry if I said something uncomfortable and—"

"It's okay," Quinn said. "I'm gay, but that's not why we're here…this is." He focused and shifted the water's path so it moved up into the air between them and then neatly flowed back down into the sink drain.

"What the hell?" Mr. St. Germain said, startled, mouth falling agape as he stared at the impossible, gravity-defying stream of water. "Are you doing that?" he whispered.

Quinn raised his hand to make it painfully obvious. The water shifted into an S-pattern as Quinn's hand moved around it. "S for Saint Germain."

"How?" Mr. St. Germain asked, flabbergasted.

Quinn dropped his hand, and the water splashed into the sink and resumed its normal flow.

"Okay," Mr. St. Germain said excitedly. "Tell me *everything*."

Twenty minutes later, the boys finished retelling their strange experience in the mysterious underground cave and their ordeal in the hospital, including the perplexing Agent Victor Kraze and the web of lies around their recovery. When they finished telling Mr. St. Germain about the phenomena they had been experiencing at home, work, and school, he started asking questions.

"So, these things happened, and you can or can't control them?" Mr. St. Germain asked.

"That's the thing," Quinn said. "At first, it's always by accident. But if I work at it, I can start to control it. Making water do things is my easiest trick."

Mr. St. Germain looked at Blake.

"I can't control anything yet," Blake said. "These things happen and I don't have the ability to control them, although last night when I got pissed at my dad, I was able to diffuse it before I burned the house down."

"How'd you do that?" Quinn asked.

"I ran down the street—like really fast—in my boxers and jumped into a neighbor's pool. I did scorch my dad's patio, though. I don't think my parents have seen it yet."

"Oh boy," Quinn said. "You ran really fast?"

"You scorched the ground?"

Blake answered Quinn first. "Yeah, like way faster than I normally run." Then he addressed Mr. St. Germain's question. "When I get hot, I create intense heat you can feel that usually scorches or burns whatever is around me, like pavement or grass."

"Did you make those round burn marks in the parking lot?"

"Maybe," Blake said.

"I saw those and wondered what had happened."

"Yeah, Darien was being a prick and he pissed me off."

"Is that the trigger? Anger?" Mr. St. Germain asked.

Quinn could tell his mind was working overtime trying to understand and explain what was going on.

"I'm not sure," Blake answered.

"Quinn, when you first realized you could make the water move in the shower, what was going on?"

"Um, I was showering?"

Mr. St. Germain chucked. "Yeah, I got that part. That's not what I meant. What I mean is, what were you thinking about, if it's appropriate for me to hear?"

"Oh." Quinn chuckled, thinking back to that morning. "It was the first morning back in my own house, the Friday we came back to school just over a week ago. I had just gotten in the shower, and I was thinking about Victor Kraze and the lies that we were being told and our parents had been told."

"Okay, Blake, when you first—"

"Wait," Quinn said. He pointed to the cabinets that held the chemistry glassware. "That was the day the beakers exploded. I think that was me. I was thinking about Keegan Miller."

"You were thinking about Keegan?" Mr. St. Germain repeated.

"He has a crush on him," Blake explained.

Quinn elbowed his buddy. "I don't need that getting around, you know."

"Sorry."

"No problem, that's one secret I can keep," Mr. St. Germain said, smiling. "Okay…um…Blake, when you maybe-sort-of burned Darien's arm and scorched the parking lot, what were you thinking about?"

"Punching him in the face, probably. He had just made one of his stupid Quinn the Queer jokes and I got pissed off."

"Wait, you got pissed off, and the heat happened?" Mr. St. Germain asked, his voice bubbling with excitement.

"I think so."

"Quinn, slightly awkward question, but what were you *feeling* when you made the water dance in the shower?"

"I was thinking about the lies and feeling very frustrated by the whole thing."

"And Blake, when you almost burned the house down last night? What were you feeling?"

"I was super irritated with my dad when he started telling me I was an idiot. I felt hurt. You'd think I'd be used to it by now, but—"

"You should never get used to being put down, Blake," Mr. St. Germain said.

"I guess not."

"That's it!" Mr. St. Germain exclaimed, clapping his hands.

"What is?" the boys said together.

"These things aren't connected to what you're necessarily thinking, but right now they're totally inspired by what's happening around you. Your budding powers, for lack of a better word, seemed to be tied to your emotions."

Quinn and Blake looked at each other. *It can't be that simple.*

"But I can control water without feeling frustrated. Wouldn't I need to feel frustrated in order to do that?"

"Not necessarily. A lot of things can impact why you can access some of your powers on demand, such as your comfortability with emotions, emotional maturity, the maturation of your powers, the powers you have available to you based on what's going on. This is obviously a completely undiscovered realm of science—"

"That's why we need your help," Quinn said emphatically. "We can't figure this out."

"Right. What were you feeling when you stopped the car?" Mr. St. Germain asked.

"I was afraid...no, I was horrified."

"And when you hovered over the ground, Blake?" Mr. St. Germain asked.

"I was surprised."

"Not scared or shocked?"

"No, it happened too fast for that." Blake took a deep breath and shifted his weight from his left foot to his right foot. "Definitely surprised."

"This explains why I almost blew up my room when I—" Quinn abruptly stopped speaking. He felt himself blush when he realized what he was about to share.

Mr. St. Germain and Blake looked at him, expecting him to continue.

Quinn shrugged and looked at Blake, making a you-should-know-what-I'm-talking-about-face. "You know!"

Blake's eyes lit up and he nodded. "Oh, right. Yeah, I noticed that, too."

"Mind letting me in on this?" Mr. St. Germain asked.

"Uh," Quinn said. "It was early morning, I was thinking about Keegan, and I, um, took matters into my own hand—"

Mr. St. Germain raised his hand. "Stop. I get it." He paused to think. "So…for both of you…feelings of arousal or lust make things…I can't believe I'm going to say this…explode?"

Quinn nodded vigorously. "That's it!"

"Yeah," Blake said sheepishly.

"Well, be careful, I guess. I'm willing to bet this is temporary until your powers—"

"Superpowers," Quinn corrected.

Mr. St. Germain laughed. "Is that what we're calling them now?"

"If we figure out how to control them, then heck yes!" Quinn said.

"What about the sensing thing?" Blake asked.

"The what?" Mr. St. Germain asked, wrinkling his brow.

"Oh, right, we forgot that part," Quinn said. He explained the strange sense of proximity they felt whenever they came into an unknown range of each other.

"Like, right now," Blake said, "I know exactly where Quinn is."

"But you can see him," Mr. St. Germain said, confused.

"No, I can mentally sense where he physically is. If he were in the next classroom, I could tell you exactly where he was standing or sitting. I could probably even guess which desk he was sitting at if I knew the layout of the classroom."

"Echolocation?" Mr. St. Germain said, mostly to himself. "Can you sense everything around you?"

"I don't know what that is, but I can only sense Quinn in relation to me. I can't sense anything or anyone else."

Mr. St. Germain shrugged as his eyes darted around the ceiling. Quinn could tell he was searching his comic-filled, encyclopedic brain for an answer. "It's just a guess, but it might be because you got these powers together. I don't have another explanation yet. You said you were holding onto each other in the cave?"

"Yeah, we were pretty scared," Quinn said, nodding.

"I thought we were gonna be electrocuted and die," Blake said.

"Well, we did die," Quinn added. "At least, that's what the hospital staff told us. That's one of the only points no one disagreed with, so I assume it's one of the few truths about what happened during those three days."

"Blake, think about Darien."

"No," Blake said.

"Trust me. Think about the parking lot, when he insulted you and Quinn. Try to remember what that felt like."

Blake frowned.

"Fine." His voice betrayed his annoyance with the idea. "He's just a relentless pain in the ass who needs to be put in his place. He bullies way too many people."

"Think about your dad last night."

Blake shook his head. "You're really trying to rev me up, aren't you?"

"Okay, stop," Mr. St. Germain said, raising his hand. "I can feel the heat coming off you. You weren't kidding. Think happy thoughts, Blake: puppies and kittens."

Blake chuckled.

"Like winning a race and beating Darien's time," Quinn said, elbowing his friend. Blake laughed, and Mr. St. Germain nodded.

"Good, you're cooling down. So, irritation or frustration makes heat. The next time something unusual happens, you need reflect about what you're feeling—very distinctly. There could be subtle differences between emotions, and you don't want to confuse the two."

"That still doesn't explain how we can control the powers," Quinn said.

"Well, that's why you came to me, right?" Mr. St. Germain asked. "Based on what you shared, your emotions trigger new powers but are not the source of your powers. I'll help you figure this out, and believe me, I won't tell a soul as long as you two aren't out there pretending to be Batman and Robin—"

"I'm not his sidekick," Blake said dryly.

"Noted."

"Batman and Robin don't have superpowers. We're more like Hancock and—" Quinn stopped and thought for a moment. "I'm not sure who else is like Hancock, except Superman."

Mr. St. Germain jumped in. "You could be like Invincible, Captain Marvel, Hyperion…there are a number of multi-power-wielding comic heroes out there. Or, you could be something completely different. That'd be tough, though, all the tropes are taken. But no matter what the comics or movies say, you could very well be the world's first superheroes, and this is your origin story."

Quinn smiled. "I like that."

"Now, the bigger question in my head is: Who's running that underground energy facility, and what are they doing with it? You guys, I suspect, were an accidental awakening—unless they already know what it can do to human biology—or you're the first to survive it. That would explain why Victor Kraze was so interested in what happened to you, and if the hospital staff were honest about calling him in for all the strange stuff, you might not have been the first to experience it."

"You mean there are others out there like us?" Quinn asked. "That's what you're saying, right?"

"It's *possible*, but I have no idea. More importantly, if there *are* other superpowered people out there, we don't know which side they're on."

"How would we even know if we met one?" Blake asked. "Better yet, would they know about us?"

"If that sensing thing you talked about extends to anyone who was dosed with cave energy, then you would sense each other." Mr. St. Germain paused and shifted his head. "Unless the ability to mask yourself from others is a superpower you could learn. Then you may never know if someone near you is superpowered or not. The exception might be you two, since you were transformed together. You may never be able to hide from each other, which means you might have no way of practicing until you discover another superpowered person—or they discover you."

"That's scary," Quinn said.

"I'm just theorizing," Mr. St. Germain said. "We don't know anything, really. Like I said, this is totally uncharted science."

"Well, thanks, Mr. St. Germain," Quinn said. "I feel better having spoken with you. At least now we can probably figure out how to control things better and not accidentally hurt others or blow things up."

"Remember, as you learn to control your superpowers—man, that's something I never thought I'd ever hear myself say—you'll develop the ability to use them better as your emotions sort out and mature. Come back whenever you have questions. I'll do some research on my own to see what I can discover that might be useful. And thank you, boys, for trusting me with this. You just have to promise me one thing."

"What's that?" Quinn said.

"Don't do anything stupid. Don't put yourself out there, don't try to be heroes by helping people. If anyone finds out about what you can do, you could ignite a shit-storm of media coverage that would only bring lots of unwanted heat down upon you guys. Besides, so far you aren't bulletproof, and you don't seem invincible yet. Both of you swear you *will not be stupid about this.*"

"I swear," Blake said.

"Me too," Quinn said. "But it's gonna be really hard not sorting this out."

"I didn't say you couldn't sort this out, just do it discreetly. Make sure you're alone and no one's watching you. You don't need someone like Darien discovering your secret. Remember what Carmine Falcone told Bruce Wayne in *Batman Begins:* 'You always fear what you don't understand.'"

Blake and Quinn looked at each other and smiled. They loved that movie, and for whatever reason, the line stuck with them and kept coming back.

"Just like in the new *Man of Steel* movie, people freaked out about Superman. They didn't trust him and the military tried to take him into custody. They will slice and dice you to figure out what makes you tick and try to control you because they're afraid you will represent their ultimate destruction."

"Why aren't you afraid of us?" Blake asked.

"Because I know you two. You're good guys, and I'm pretty sure world domination isn't one of your aspirations. Am I wrong?"

"Nope," the boys said together.

"All right, then. Get out of here before my head explodes. I have no superpower to prevent me from being distracted with this for the rest of the day."

The bell rang as the boys thanked him again and headed off to their next class.

Chapter 13
Darkness Rising

Blake

"See you later, buddy. Try not to burn anything in your boredom," Quinn teased, snapping his helmet straps together after school. Then, he pedaled away.

Blake smiled and waved. "Have fun at work, and don't worry, Portsmouth will be safe today, I promise." Blake watched his friend pedal away for a moment before pulling on his backpack. He swung his leg over his bicycle, strapped his helmet on, and looked around. Most of his teammates had already left after track practice, and those with cars were heading home or to their jobs. He took a deep breath, exhaled, then pushed off and cycled away from the high school.

Several minutes later, Blake pedaled down Court Street, his running tank top flapping in the wind. He steered his bicycle through Prescott Park until he rode across the Peirce Island Bridge and found himself turning left onto the raised path that brought him to the park and picnic areas on Four Tree Island. He jumped off his bike and walked it to one of the park's covered picnic spots and rested it against the picnic table. He pulled off his helmet and backpack and set them down next to his bike. A number of roofed picnic areas dotted the perimeter of the small island, and at its center, a large, grassy field offered enjoyment for everyone. He sat on the picnic table and rested his feet on the seat in front of him.

At last, peace and quiet.

Although it had been an unusually stressful school day, he was glad their talk with Mr. St. Germain garnered insight about their developing abilities. Still, he knew he had to be careful about how much he shared with Quinn and Mr. St. Germain because they would not appreciate what he wanted to do with his superpowers. For the first time, he realized he would have to keep secrets from his best friend.

Blake stared across the churning Piscataqua River at the Portsmouth Naval Shipyard, a busy submarine repair and refit station. His vision provided incredible clarity, and the sounds of various machinery reached his oversensitive ears. Today, a second submarine was parked against the exposed docks, but he couldn't see how many were parked in the large, dry dock building. He decided to sit for a while because the water's edge was a great place to think and he didn't want to go home and face his angry father again. He had no idea how they would pay off the expensive hospital bills they'd received.

Focusing on the passing water of the river, he quieted his mind and reduced the enhanced loudness of the shipyard and other sounds around him. Although Portsmouth was on the river and not the ocean, the harbor and river waters were tidal, and the faint smell of salt water filled his nose. Blake found something rejuvenating about the smell of salt water combined with the afternoon sun he couldn't explain. At the moment, however, low tide challenged his sense of smell with the sun-baked odors of drying seaweed, dead fish, and other unpleasant scents he could not identify.

Behind him, two girls giggled under one of the covered picnic spots. He glanced at them, but they were caught up in their own world, enjoying something on their phones. He returned his gaze to the river and watched several fishing boats navigate to the docks on the left side of the island. Several deep breaths later, his thoughts returned to his new, superpowered ambitions.

If I'm not going to be Quinn's sidekick, what does that mean for me? What exactly am I going to be if I use my powers differently from Quinn?

He shifted his butt on the table and stretched his back before resting his elbows on his knees, his chin on his clasped hands. *Quinn totally wants to do the Superman thing and save people who need rescuing and all that stuff, but that's not what I want to do.*

"Hey, ladies, mind if we join you?" a man asked loudly. The roughness of his voice broke through Blake's focus. *I hope I get this under control soon.*

"No thanks," they said. Blake glanced over his shoulder and saw two men sauntering across the grassy field toward the girls. He felt himself tense up, instinctively knowing something was very wrong with them. One man was tall and heavily tattooed, and the other was medium height with fewer tattoos. Both wore pants, white tank tops, and larger-than-necessary gold chains around their necks that hung low on their chests. The shorter guy held a brown paper bag in his hand that looked as if it contained a bottle of liquor.

Aw, shit. A sinking feeling descended over Blake as he realized he might have to intervene before the situation turned ugly.

"What's the matter, don't you want to party with us?" the tall one said. "Sun's out, great breeze, and you fine ladies look like you need some fun company. That's us!"

"No thanks," the girls said, their voices more insistent and annoyed.

The men were not deterred. "Come on," the short one pleaded, his voice betraying irritation. "We'll have a lot of fun, I promise. I know this because you're really beautiful girls."

I don't think those guys have seen me yet. They don't know I'm here.

Blake pulled his legs and feet up and turned himself around, resting his feet on the picnic seat that faced the inside of the picnic area so he could better see what was going on. He looked around for help but didn't see anyone else on the island. There were no signs of life on the mainland or on Peirce Island, either.

Shit, I'm gonna have to deal with this…unless I just leave…

"Leave us alone, please," one of the girls said, her voice now nervous and upset.

"But we want to have fun with you tonight," Short Man said, his voice slurred.

"Jake, can you help us, please?" she asked, looking at Blake.

Blake didn't move. He straightened up and pointed at himself. *Is she talking to me?*

The girl nodded emphatically. "Yes, Jake, you. Could you come over here, please? Now?"

Blake stood, and the two guys turned around and glared at him, their eyes full of anger.

"Well, well, what have we here, Jake? One of Portsmouth's finest? Go Clippers, my ass," Tall Man said, smirking at Blake's track tank top. Short Man laughed wickedly, and Blake immediately regretted not changing after track practice. His tank top identified his last name, team number, and the school he attended.

Blake slowly walked a wide circle around the men, keeping his front to them so they wouldn't see his last name. He made his way to the girls' picnic table. He felt scared and didn't know if the two men would walk away or try to take him out. Short Man took a swig from the paper-bag-covered bottle and passed it to Tall Man, who took a longer swig. He wiped his mouth with the back of his hand and jeered at Blake.

"Why don't you take your pretty face and run it out of here, jockey-poo," Tall Man said, putting on an effeminate accent.

"It's Jake," Short Man said, drunkenly correcting his friend. Then he spoke to Blake, "We don't want to have to hurt you, so beat it, kid."

Blake took a deep breath and exhaled slowly. *There's no way I'm getting out of this mess now.*

"I'm sorry, I can't do that. The ladies told you they didn't want to hang out with you—"

"That's just too damn bad," Tall Man slurred, swiping his hand across the open space in front of his chest.

"You need to leave," Blake said loudly, trying to assert himself as the situation deteriorated. "Just leave the park and go away."

"And how are you gonna make us leave, Jake?" Tall Man asked, stepping forward with a menacing glare in his eyes. He passed the bottle back to his short friend, who chuckled.

Blake turned to the girls. "Get out of here and don't look back. Call the police when you're safe in Prescott Park."

"Oh my gosh, thank you, Jake," one of the girls said, and they grabbed their belongings. "You need to get out of here before they hurt you."

"Yup, I will." Blake nodded at them.

"Thank you so much, if you weren't here, we could be—"

"Jake, you're ruining our fun, you little pisser," the short man yelled.

"Don't go," the tall man loudly pleaded. He stepped toward the girls, but Blake stepped in front of him, cutting him off. The two drunk men hesitated, unsure of what they should do.

Blake watched the girls hustle away and make their way back to Peirce Island. He decided not to correct the thugs about his name in case they told someone about what happened. If they kept using the wrong name, no one would be able to connect him to what was about to happen.

Now, step forward, show them who's boss. You can take these two jerks out, they're drunk.

Blake stepped forward and stared into the tall guy's eyes. "You wanna play with someone, asshole? Then let's play right now." He felt his adrenaline surge with a fight reaction as the power behind his eyes blazed.

"What the hell?" the short man said, pointing at Blake's eyes.

Then the drunk tall man coiled his arm back with surprising speed. "Fuck you, you little prick!"

This is gonna hurt!

Tall Man's right hook slammed into Blake's jaw, impacting the flesh and bone with a strange *thwuck*. The force of the blow barely turned Blake's head. His jaw hurt a little, but not like it should have.

Tall Man screamed in agony, clutching his right hand with his left. "What the fuck?" he yelled, falling to his knees. "You almost broke my hand!"

"You little punk," Short Man snarled.

Blake became irritated with them and felt his body temperature slowly rising. He reached up and felt his jaw, which, surprisingly, didn't hurt.

Short Man sidestepped and then jumped forward, slightly off balance but ready to attack. Blake saw his opening. When Short Man pulled his arm back, Blake's left arm sprang up and forward. He delivered a swift uppercut that slammed the man's jaw shut as his head rolled back. His hands and arms moved out to his sides as the man fell backwards, landing on his back with a thud.

Blake looked at his left hand, which should have hurt. Instead, he only felt heat radiating from his body as the grass around him scorched.

Tall Man pushed himself off the ground and staggered toward Blake. "I'll cut you," he said, fishing for something in his pocket with his right hand.

Knife!

"No, I don't think so," Blake said. He jumped toward the man, ready to strike. The man was faster and raised the knife.

Shit!

Blake tried to sidestep left but couldn't dodge the jabbing knife. It struck him on the right side of his abdomen, and he stopped. Blake's eyes opened wide as he froze in place. He didn't know what being stabbed felt like, but the sharp pain on his right side gave him a significant clue. *Oh no!*

The man snarled and laughed at the same time.

Blake looked down and saw the tip of the knife pressing against his track shirt. "Why didn't you stab me?" Blake asked, panicked.

"What?" the man asked, surprised. He looked at his right hand and the knife. He pulled it back and jabbed it forward again, aiming for the center of Blake's torso.

Blake felt a sharp pinch where the tip of the knife touched his body. Though it pressed against his running shirt, it did not seem to penetrate his skin.

Oh wow, because you can't...I'm knife-proof!

Blake smiled, his eyes blazing orange. The man looked at him with fear in his eyes and stepped back. Blake moved with him and landed a right hook to the man's temple. Tall Man's eyes rolled up as he fell to the ground like a tree that had just been cut.

Timber!

He turned to face the unconscious men and felt himself becoming angry. "I'm going to make you pay for what you tried to do," Blake said as anger filled his veins, the familiar sensation of intense heat rising in his body. He looked back for the girls but didn't see them or anyone else. Remembering how his boxers had nearly burned at the family fight, he pulled off his tank top and gym shorts and tossed them about ten feet away. He examined his skin where the knife had made contact, but there was no blood or stab wound.

Fantastic!

Standing in his boxer shorts, he squatted low and pointed a hand toward each man, hoping his running shoes and socks could take the heat. *I have no idea if this works this way, but you guys totally deserve to get burned for what you were about to do.*

He focused.

The heat surged through his body, and he relaxed, allowing the heat to radiate away from his body. Within seconds, the grass around him wilted and the exposed skin on the men became pink, taking on the appearance of a bad sunburn.

If I see you losers again, I'll make you suffer far worse than a mild sunburn.

Blake took a deep breath and stood. He felt the power behind his eyes fade. He looked around, then jogged over to his track clothes. He pulled on his shorts and looked around again, but he still saw no one. The girls had just cleared the walkway gate on Peirce Island and popped into view, so he ran over to his bike and backpack and shoved his tank top into the waistband of his shorts. He didn't want anyone to see his name or team number.

He pulled his backpack on and then jumped onto his bike as soon as it cleared the picnic table. He pedaled past the two unconscious men and flipped them the bird as his bike changed gears and he made his way across the walkway.

When he crossed the Peirce Island Bridge, he turned right and made his way through Prescott Park. People relaxed on benches or walked through the park. None of them, apparently, had seen him wield his powers. Behind him, two police cars, lights and sirens blazing, made their way onto Peirce Island. He assumed the girls had called 911, and now he was glad to be away from the scene.

He thought about going to the coffee shop to see Quinn, but it was early evening and he knew his buddy wouldn't be able to get away from the customers to chat. Since he wasn't ready to go home, he decided to pedal around Portsmouth for a while.

Blake walked downstairs to the kitchen, lost in his thoughts. He hadn't seen his father yet, but his mother acted like nothing had happened the night before.

When he'd arrived home earlier in the evening, he'd checked the patio and seen that the whole thing had darkened in color; there wasn't an obvious circle like there was in the school parking lot or the baseball field. Some of the grass on the edges had wilted, but it didn't look scorched. He shrugged, and after silently eating dinner with his mom, he went to his room to do homework and play a game on his Xbox.

When it was eleven o'clock, he shut down the game console and went downstairs into the kitchen to get some water and say goodnight to his mother, who was watching the local news. When he finished filling his glass, the news anchor from WMUR News Nine caught his attention. He walked into the living room to listen.

"This evening, police were alerted and responded to a call regarding two drunken men fighting on Four Tree Island in Portsmouth tonight. When police arrived at the scene, they found the men, both from Massachusetts, lying on the ground, unconscious with severe sunburns on their skin. While a knife was found near one of the men, no stab wounds were found. Both men had taken punches to the face, but paramedics found no other injuries related to the apparent fight they had. Police confirmed liquor was a factor, and the men have been charged with drunken and disorderly conduct. They will remain in the Portsmouth jail overnight until next-of-kin can be contacted. In other news…"

Blake smiled. *Damn, it felt good to make those guys pay for their stupidity.*

"Good night, Mom," he said, turning back toward the stairs.

"Night, Blake," she answered, not looking away from the television.

Blake made his way back to his room and shut the door. He turned out the light and then pulled off his shirt and gym shorts and sat on the edge of his bed.

So, my secret is safe. I can't tell Quinn any of this. Well, I can tell him about the invincible part…but if he finds out I used my powers to hurt those guys, he'll go ballistic and I'll never hear the end of it. Maybe that's the difference between us, though.

Quinn wants to use his powers to help people. That's all well and good, but somebody has to make these jerks pay for their crimes. I can do that. I can become something they fear, like Batman, who bruises and maims when necessary…but I'll take it up a notch by torturing and breaking them…

Maybe that's the problem these days: hardened criminals don't fear the justice system…

Maybe they'll fear the guy who can hurt them…

Maybe they'll fear the one man they can't stop...

Maybe they'll fear a little...injustice...

Blake grinned widely and stared at his reflection in the mirror above his dresser. He tilted his head down until he could barely see his eyes under his eyebrows, summoning a darker version of himself that would find strength and confidence in his unique brand of justice.

His eyes glowed orange for a moment, and he smiled.

He sniggered and then settled into bed, pulling the covers over his waist as his head rested on one of his pillows. It was warm in his room, but not warm enough to run the air conditioner in his window. He closed his eyes and inhaled, exhaling slowly as he waited for sleep to come.

I'll be the one to make them pay, to make them suffer when they think they've gotten away with murder, or worse.

Chapter 14

Normal is Upside Down

Quinn

Quinn grinned as the wind rushed past his face, his fingers playing in the breeze as he effortlessly flew through the air, zipping around the bridges of Portsmouth as people pointed at him from the ground. He laughed, blasting his way across the river's surface while leaving a mixed wake of air and salt water behind him as he soared upriver toward Dover, looping around the Little Bay Bridges a few times. He flew upward, hovering about two hundred feet above the bay with Dover on his left and Portsmouth on his right.

"Eat your heart out, Superman!" Quinn yelled to the open air.

"Maybe I will," a voice behind him answered.

"What?" Quinn whipped around and came face to face with Superman.

"You're *real?*" Quinn sputtered, too stunned.

"Of course."

"But you're a DC Comics creation!"

Superman laughed. "Where do you think the comics get their inspiration from?" He pointed at Quinn, then jerked a thumb back to himself. "They get them from us, real-life superheroes, of course."

Quinn nodded, confused.

Superman smiled and started to drift away. "Make sure you use your powers for good. I wouldn't want to have to put you down, Quinn. Okay?"

"Yes," Quinn stuttered.

"All right then. Take care!"

Quinn blinked, and Superman was gone. He twisted around again, looking for the man in blue and red, but he found himself alone, hovering in the air. Suddenly, he plummeted through the air, unable to stop himself from falling.

I don't want to die!

Quinn's eyes popped open as he gasped for air. He tried to sit up, but he whacked his head on something big and white.

"Ouch! What the heck?" he exclaimed.

Quinn's eyes focused in the darkness of his bedroom, and he found himself floating a mere six inches from the flat white paint of his ceiling. Stunned, he turned his head and twisted his shoulders to look down at his bed.

I can fly?

Suddenly, the bed rushed toward him as gravity pulled him down. He bounced on the bed, which protested his unexpected landing with a muffled creaking sound.

He chuckled and sat up, rubbing his eyes. Then, he pushed himself up, and his body hovered in the air.

I can fly!

He grinned with excitement, his mind concocting a wild idea. He allowed himself to descend to the bed. He tiptoed to his closet and pulled out some black track pants and a navy-blue sweatshirt. Shoving his feet into some sneakers, he snuck downstairs and out of the house. Quinn quietly latched the back door to the house and tiptoed down the asphalt driveway. At two o'clock in the morning, it was unusually bright outside. A full moon lit the night sky with a blue hue around him.

When he was far enough from the house and out of earshot, he jogged to the Sagamore Creek Bridge on Route 1A. Several cars went by, but at that hour, most of Portsmouth was fast asleep. When Quinn reached the bridge, he looked around to make sure no one was watching. Then, he grabbed the metal railing and jumped over it.

The rush of air on his face invigorated him as he spread his hands and legs, willing himself to level off and move forward, inches from the water's surface.

Then, he flew.

All he had to do was think about where he wanted to go and how fast he wanted to get there, and his body responded, moving through the air with swiftness and grace.

Boat docks whizzed past as he made his way toward the Wentworth by the Sea hotel, laughing to himself as he flew up and around it, arms spread back like a fighter jet. Strangely, the cool wind whipping at his face didn't bother his eyes. He circled the famous hotel and dove down toward the water, accelerating over the Piscataqua River as he whipped through the slalom of islands. He could see everything around him in exquisite detail, despite the dark hour. For a moment, he assumed it was the moonlight, but he smiled when he realized it was his enhanced vision. Assuming his eyes were glowing, he leveled out at two feet above sea level and increased his speed, flying upriver, keeping to the New Hampshire side of the river to avoid tripping any motion sensors at the Portsmouth Naval Shipyard.

Following the course of an imaginary cargo ship and leaving a small wake behind him in the churning, powerful waters of the Piscataqua, Quinn flew under the drawbridges and made his way to the massive, green-arched Piscataqua River Bridge.

Quinn looked toward Atlantic Heights, where Blake lived. *I hope I don't trip our sensing thing…maybe if I keep my distance, it won't happen.*

When he flew under the bridge deck, he willed himself upward and soared to the crown of the bridge. At nearly three hundred feet above sea level, Quinn alighted on the steel arch bridge near the flashing white light. He sat down on the apex, his legs dangling over the edge. In front of him, the tidal Piscataqua River and the night lights of Portsmouth and Kittery, Maine, disappeared into the darkness of the unlit ocean in the not-so-far distance.

I can fly!

He shifted to the inside of the massive steel beam and looked down and watched the late-night traffic on the interstate below him, seeing car colors with incredible detail. Then, his eyes locked onto a familiar red car. Even though he sat almost two hundred feet above the road deck, he recognized the make and model of a red car that matched the one that had almost clobbered that kid and his mother.

His mind flashed back to Daniel Street…the mother, the toddler, the brief squeal of tires, the loud bang, the airbag, the crunching metal…the man he almost killed.

His mood immediately soured as he thought of the near-fatal accident. *Is it worth flying if I almost get someone killed? As cool as the powers are…something's going to go wrong eventually. Tonight, it was simply flying, but what if I explode something…or someone…by accident?*

"We need to go back," Quinn said, testing the waters with his friend.

"What? Go back where?" Blake asked.

The boys were playing *Halo* on Quinn's Xbox together after school. Neither of them had track practice or work that day.

"To Rangeley, where all this started. To that cave."

"Do you seriously think our parents would let us go up there again, after everything that happened?" Blake asked. "My father would kill me, or at least try to. The last thing we need is another hospital bill."

Quinn swallowed nervously. "I know that, which is why we'd have to…lie."

Blake nearly dropped his controller when the word came out of Quinn's mouth. "*You* want to lie to your dads?"

Quinn paused the game as Blake looked at his best friend, a shocked expression on his face. "We're already lying about a lot," Quinn said sheepishly. He lowered his controller and met Blake's gaze. "We're lying about being normal when we're the first superpowered people on the planet—that we know of."

"True." Blake looked at the floor, unsure of what to say. "I mean, we—"

"What if we could go back and reverse what was done to us?"

"Reverse it?" Blake exclaimed, a bit louder than he expected. "Quinn, you can *fly*. Why on earth would you want to undo *this*?" He held out his hand, palm up, and the controller levitated upward and slowly rotated clockwise. *I am not going to give up my powers, not even for you.*

Quinn's mouth dropped open in surprise. "When did you figure that out?"

"This morning. When I went to get coffee in the kitchen before showering, I reached for the mug and it slid across the counter to my hand."

"No way! That's awesome!"

"Yes way. I put the mug back and did it again. I spent the entire morning practicing, and you know what the best part is?"

"No, what?" Quinn said, a grin spreading across his face. Suddenly, the controller in his hand floated up as well.

"I can control it."

"Finally!" Quinn said, laughing. He grabbed the game controller from the air and flipped it around in his hand.

"So, what is it you can do, exactly?" Quinn asked, shifting on the couch to face Blake.

"I can move things around, basically."

"There's a word for that, but I can't think of it. Magneto does it, but—"

"He can only manipulate metals. My coffee mug had no metal in it. Neither did my shower towel, the shampoo bottle, or the comic books I practiced with."

"So, just little things?"

"Well, that's all I practiced on. I haven't tried to move a car or anything yet."

"Wow," Quinn said, sitting back on the couch, watching Blake's floating controller. Then he frowned as his excitement deflated as quickly as it had inflated.

"I know this is awesome and stuff, but still I want to undo this. I want to be normal. I don't want to be the guy whose powers accidentally hurt people."

"Oh my gosh, Quinn! Are you still stuck on this? I thought we had just talked you off the ledge with having these abilities. You will *never* be the guy who intentionally hurts people. The minute you have a better grip on your powers, you'll be out there playing *Superhero Boy Wonder*." Blake made air quotes around the nickname.

"Okay, that's never going to be my code name."

Blake laughed. "Good, because it's terrible."

Quinn sighed as Blake continued.

"What was the point of talking with Mr. St. Germain if you want to undo this? Assuming we even *can* undo this. We got zapped with that energy stuff. Are you thinking about trying to get zapped again? I'm pretty sure that would only strengthen our powers, not take them away."

Quinn thought for a moment. "You're probably right."

"Besides, we could barely recover from the first dose of energy. If a second dose is as equally lethal, we'll end up back in the hospital, and Victor Kraze will be all over us."

"Ugh, I just want to be normal," Quinn said, throwing himself back onto the couch. He dropped his controller in his lap and rubbed his temples with the palms of his hands.

Blake became exasperated. "You still haven't convinced me. What is so damn awesome about being normal? Adults get annoyed with teenagers when we defy normal and try to push the boundaries whenever we can. Now you just want to sit back and not do that?"

"Pretty much, yeah. I want to be like everyone else, don't you?"

"Well, buddy, you're not like everyone else. You haven't been normal since you realized you were gay and—"

"What?" Quinn said, his face contorted with hurt and confusion.

"You're gay."

"I know that. This isn't 1950; being gay isn't abnormal," Quinn spat angrily.

Blake shook his head. "Sorry, that's not what I meant at all. Come on, bud, you know me better than that."

Quinn nodded. "Okay."

"Think about it, though. You have two dads, who, last time I checked, are gay. I think that's awesome, but it's different around here. So you don't have normal in your life and haven't had it for a long time. Until same-sex parents are widely regarded as *normal*, whatever that means in this case, you have a very nontraditional—but wonderful—family model. My alcoholic family isn't normal either, with my alcoholic father and my functionally alcoholic and enabling mother. I'm the scapegoat for everything they mess up. We are already *not* normal by a long shot."

Quinn's brows furled.

"Careful," Blake said, raising his hand in caution. "Let's not accidentally burn the house down."

Quinn laughed and nodded. "Yeah. You're right. Frustration tends to bring out the scorching heat superpowers."

"Look, Quinn, we cannot…not have these powers. They're only going to get stronger, and hopefully we'll be able to control them better. The only way we get to be normal is by trying not to use the powers and live like normal people, just like we did before. We figure them out, get them under control, and if you still want to be normal, don't use them."

Quinn sighed. "I know, you're right. I'm having a hard time accepting it."

"Maybe if you came out to your dads, things would be easier for you because there'd be one less thing for you to hide. I mean, seriously, think about it this way: if you've got one *normal gay thing* going for you, it's the whole same-sex parents thing. Your dads will still love you, and outside of the jerks like Darien, no one at school will care. Besides, if you were out of the closet, I'm sure a certain Keegan Miller might take a newfound interest in you."

Quinn smiled and sat forward. "You think so?"

"You're not out, Quinn. It's not his job to push you out of the closet."

Quinn nodded and readied his control. "All right, all right. I get the point. I still want to go back to Rangeley. We need more information."

Blake sighed.

"If we can at least understand what it is, Mr. St. Germain can help us figure out *how* this happened. We'll take our phones, take pictures, gather evidence. We can even go check out that museum Dr. Madison talked about."

"And if we bump into Victor?"

Quinn shrugged. "Well, um…I don't know. We just make up an excuse. We'll think of something."

"Okay, fine."

"Good. Now that we have that settled, let's keep playing the game so I can kick your ass."

"Never gonna happen," Blake quipped.

Quinn chuckled, and the game resumed.

Chapter 15

Return to the Source

Quinn

Quinn pulled the SUV into the empty Woods Lake Campground parking lot and shut off the engine. He looked over at Blake, who had fallen asleep an hour ago.

"Hey," he said, elbowing him gently.

"I'm awake," Blake said, startled.

"We're here," Quinn said, chuckling.

"Right, okay." Blake wiped his eyes and stretched in the car seat. "Sorry, didn't mean to conk out on you."

"It's okay." Quinn looked around. Leaves had already started turning in the cooler days and nights that Rangeley experienced in autumn. Though many tourists would travel far to see the vibrant colors, locals knew the turning of the leaves meant the arrival of snow in the months to come.

"I'm ready," Blake said.

"I think we need to agree on something first," Quinn said, shutting off the engine.

"What's that?"

"Let's not use our powers."

"Why? It's not like I can without getting pissed off or something," Blake said.

Quinn could tell Blake was upset at his latent abilities. "If anyone up here knows what's going on, I don't want to tip them off that their cave thingy gave us abilities. We don't need to raise anyone's suspicions."

Blake nodded. "Agreed. Okay, let's do this."

The boys got out of the SUV and made their way to the cargo space at the back. Quinn grabbed the backpack of supplies they'd brought with them: a couple of super-bright LED flashlights, several bottles of electrolyte-filled water, climbing rope, and snacks.

He pulled the backpack on and then walked back to the driver side and put a note on the dashboard that read *Gone Hiking* with the date.

"Why'd you do that?" Blake asked.

"Look around," Quinn said. "No one's here. If something happens to us, they need to know we're out here. Besides, this place looks closed for the season. If the police come by, I don't want them to tow the SUV. We'd be screwed."

"Good point. As long as we're home in time for dinner and don't raise our parents' suspicions, we'll be good."

Quinn nodded and sighed. He didn't like lying to his parents, but the boys agreed they didn't have a choice. They had to find out what was going on, and they had to do it before 6 p.m., when Quinn would normally be home from track practice for dinner. Since he had the day off, Blake had called in sick to work, and the boys played hooky from school to explore the cave in more detail. Thankfully, it wasn't unusual for Quinn to take the SUV to school occasionally since Daddio would happily ferry Dad to and from his law firm. They'd probably have a lunch date together if Dad could pull himself away from clients for an hour.

Quinn locked the SUV, and the boys made their way around the campground, following signage that directed them to the trailhead.

"It smells different," Blake commented.

"Yup," Quinn answered. The scent of summer in the woods had been replaced with the slow decay of leaves mixing with earth and the dying underbrush of the forest. "Looks different too."

No rain had fallen in several days, and the forest floor, though damp in spots, was mostly dry. Their hiking boots gently thudded along the leaf-covered trail. Nature chirped and buzzed around them as several chipmunks squeaked their displeasure and scampered into the underbrush.

Thirty minutes went by, and the boys continued hiking.

"Something's not right," Blake said. "I don't recognize this part of the trail at all."

"We haven't gone past the trees yet. Remember? There's that huge line of fallen pine trees we followed."

"I'm telling you, we've passed it. It's back there," Blake insisted.

Quinn looked around. Blake was right, the forest didn't look familiar. "How did we *both* miss that? It was so obvious before." He looked ahead shrugged. "Let's go ten minutes more in this direction."

"Okay, but I'm telling you we passed it."

Five minutes later, the boys turned around.

"Told you, so," Blake said, grinning.

"Yeah, yeah. Let's keep our eyes open for the trees this time. We can't be far from it."

Several minutes later, Quinn stopped. "Look," he said, pointing up at an oak tree.

"What? Oh!" Blake exclaimed. Several of the lower limbs had been snapped off, and several broken limbs halfway up the tree hung precariously, defying gravity while daring the next big gust of wind to send them crashing to the ground.

"Something hit those," Quinn said. He started looking around for the fallen pine trees but didn't see any.

"This is definitely the spot we left the trail," Blake said, extending his arm and pointing into the woods. "Look, this whole line of trees is just…missing…like someone just scooped a straight line of trees right out of the forest."

Quinn stepped over to Blake and looked down his arm. Suddenly, the missing row of trees became embarrassingly obvious to him. He gasped. "Oh wow, you're right!" He looked around again. "Wait, the trees are gone!"

Blake nodded, his face awash with disbelief. "I think they cut them up and got rid of them."

Quinn nodded. "That's definitely weird, because I've seen storm-fallen trees stay in the woods for years. You know what's creepier, though? Who's the *they?*"

"I have no idea," Blake said. "But I bet Victor Kraze knows."

A feeling of unease settled over Quinn. "Should we leave?" *Now I'm not sure if I want to go through with this.*

"Dude, we didn't drive three and a half hours up here to turn around and drive three and a half hours back to Portsmouth empty-handed. We've got a couple hours up here, at most."

"You're right, you're right. This is just getting weirder, that's all. Okay, let's go. You know where this is? I don't want to get lost this time. It's not as easy to see where things are this time."

"All we have to do is follow the empty row of trees back to the trail. We won't get lost, I promise."

"Okay," Quinn said. "Let's do it."

Blake led the way again as the best friends retraced their steps through the forest, occasionally seeing small, straight lines of fresh sawdust. "Looks like they put tarps down wherever they could to minimize the sawdust and leave no evidence behind."

"Whoever *they* is did a really good job," Quinn said. "You can tell people have been walking around, though, there's all kinds of tramped leaves and ferns. They might have been careful to remove the trees, but they were careless with their presence."

Victor

"Sir," a security guard said, knocking at the open door. "One of the new motion sensors has been tripped. We're going to check it out, but I thought you'd like to know. Looks like a couple of teenagers are exploring the woods again."

Victor Kraze looked up from the laptop he was working on. "Two teenagers?"

"Yes, two boys."

"Do you have them on video?"

"I believe so. One of the new tree cameras we installed detected the motion."

"Don't do anything. Show me the video feed first." Victor stood and followed the guard to the security room across the hall from his office.

"Back up tree-cam four's footage by five minutes," the guard instructed the one manning the complex security system.

"Sure."

Moments later, two bodies zipped backward in reverse. Then, normal playback resumed, and they watched two teenagers pass by the hidden tree camera.

"Can you zoom in on their faces?" Victor asked.

"Yup." The guard at the console tapped a few buttons, and the video feed looped back and replayed, zooming in and focusing on the boys' faces.

Victor smiled when he recognized Quinn and Blake. "Tell everyone to stand down. I need to see what these boys are capable of, and I want no interference of any kind. Let them go wherever they want. If any of your personnel sees them, they are to ignore them and go the other way. If they bump into them, they should play nice and tell the boys to scram but not chase them away or bring them in. Keep the cameras rolling, though. I'll be watching from my office."

"Sir, what about the conversion chamber?"

"You heard me," Victor snapped.

The two guards looked at each other and shrugged. One of them picked up a radio and began relaying instructions to the other security teams.

Victor turned and walked back to his desk, the corner of his lip pulling upward.

Excellent...

Quinn

Several minutes later, the boys made it to the end of the fallen line of trees and stopped. Quinn looked left and pointed. "There's the entrance."

The lichen- and moss-covered concrete tunnel entrance, with its weathered *Keep Out* sign, looked just like he remembered.

"Still not meant for us," Blake said, smiling wickedly. "Right?"

"Of course not. Here, grab some flashlights." Quinn turned his back to Blake, who reached over and unzipped the backpack. After pulling out two LED flashlights, he zipped the backpack up and handed one to Quinn.

Quinn instinctively checked his cell phone; it had no service. "Ready?" he asked, feigning a smile. *I'm having second thoughts about this, but as long as I'm with you, I'll be okay.*

Blake winked at him. "Come on, chicken." The boys walked down the stairs and made their way into the tunnel. This time, their super-bright flashlights illuminated the tunnel and exposed all the creepy-looking roots, cracks, and water seepage they had missed from their first trip into the tunnel using only Blake's cell phone flashlight.

"Nobody must know this is out here," Quinn whispered.

"Why?"

"There's no graffiti anywhere in here. Nor is there any on the concrete box thing."

"Good point."

As they walked over the old wooden ties that connected the rails of the mining car tracks, the tunnel's darkness settled in behind them. The air became cooler as the boys descended toward the familiar metal door that led into the strange chamber, their flashlights illuminating the way.

"I don't hear it this time," Blake whispered over his shoulder.

"Hear what?" Quinn hissed.

"Remember last time, all that thrumming machinery?"

"That's right. The silence makes it more ominous," Quinn said, shivering briefly.

Moments later, the large, rusting door blocked their path. The boys turned off their flashlights, and Blake pulled on the door knob. With a faint scratching sound, it opened. A dim blue light illuminated the room. They stepped in cautiously, looking around for signs of life. When they saw none, Blake clicked on his flashlight and Quinn let go of the door. The old door-closer hissed as it pulled the door shut behind them.

"It still looks like Cerebro," Quinn said, pointing his unlit flashlight to the ceiling of the geometric chamber. At the center of the dome, the glowing blue-white ring on the conical silver thing with the three upside-down antenna arrays looked like it was off, but he could see faint pulses of blue-white light fan outward across the top of the dome and travel down the walls in the eight translucent tubes built in between the hexagonal panels that covered the sides of the octagonal chamber.

"Is this low-power mode or something?" Blake asked.

"Let's find out," Quinn said. He walked over to the hatch in the floor and pulled it open. He shined his light down into the hole and then climbed down. "This is where those battery-looking things were."

"I'll wait here," Blake said.

When his foot hit solid ground, he stepped off the ladder and turned around. Instead of a plethora of green lights, only sparse red lights shone in the darkness. The tubes from the chamber above were barely providing any illumination. He clicked on his flashlight and swung it around the large room. He walked over to a battery and studied the readout.

"If they are batteries, I think they're totally drained or barely recharged," Quinn said, loud enough for his voice to carry up through the hatch to Blake. "All of the batteries have red lights. Before, they all had lots of green lights. I think that indicates their charge status."

"I wonder how long it takes this thing to charge?" Blake asked.

Quinn shrugged, as if he were face-to-face with Blake. "No clue. There's nothing down here but these battery things. I don't see any other doors or trap doors, so, uh, I'm coming back up." He pocketed his flashlight and climbed back up the ladder to the main floor of the cavern.

"I wonder if we drained it when we got zapped?"

"Well," Quinn said, exploring what he could see in the strange chamber with his flashlight, "it was a lethal dose of zap. If they hadn't resuscitated us, we'd be dead."

"You think they do this to other people?"

Quinn shook his head and smiled, his wild imagination coming alive with possibilities "I think they were interested in us *because* we survived. I'm going to guess they didn't blast anyone yet…but obviously I don't have a clue. I agree with Mr. St. Germain—I think we were an accident."

"Interesting theory."

"There's only one way to find out," Quinn said, smiling wickedly. He shined his light on the other door in the chamber.

"Let's go see what's on the other side. I bet it's a secret control room?" Quinn asked, becoming giddy.

"Or another tunnel."

Quinn chuckled. He crossed the room, swinging the light around the door. Just like the one they came through, it needed to be pushed open from inside the chamber. "Let's kill the lights. I'll see if I can push it open first."

"Okay."

Then the boys clicked off their flashlights and listened for a moment. Using the dim blue light of the chamber, Blake walked over to Quinn. When Quinn was satisfied his enhanced hearing heard no voices on the other side, he put his hand and shoulder on the door and gently pushed. The door didn't budge.

"Gotta push harder," he whispered.

Blake nodded in the darkness.

Quinn pushed harder and felt the door move.

"Nice," Blake whispered. "Nice and easy."

Quinn pushed, and the door slowly opened…half an inch, an inch, an inch and a half, two inches, three inches, four inches. Quinn stopped and listened. There were still no sounds. He peered through the open door and saw more rock. He pushed the door open more and stuck his head through the opening.

The room was empty.

Jackpot.

He pushed the door open and stepped through it, Blake close behind. "It *is* a control room of some kind," Quinn said.

"Whaddaya know?" Blake commented. He clicked on his flashlight and started swinging the beam of light around from object to object.

Quinn did the same and stopped on a bank of old-looking beige computer banks, complete with blinking lights and large data tapes, stacked to one side of the room against a gray cinderblock wall.

"How do they keep these things running?" Quinn said, walking over to one of the refrigerator-sized computer banks.

"They must have bought all the spare parts," Blake teased.

"Seriously, is this high-tech place running off ancient computer technology?"

He shined his light over a bank of dials with various metrics; next to it was a bank with two magnetic data tapes in standby mode—according to the yellow indicator bubble. Next to that sat three banks with rows upon rows of quarter-inch jack outlets, each with red and green light bulbs. Only the third bank had old, cloth-covered wires connecting various outlets with no discernible rhyme or reason. Two smaller banks with unfamiliar dials and knobs sat next to those.

"All of these, uh, ancient computers have power. This place is still running," Quinn said softly.

"Those are computers?" Blake asked, whipping his light back and forth on the monstrous boxes.

Quinn shrugged. "Maybe they're all parts to one computer, but I don't know. I wasn't born when these things were built." He turned around and shined his light on the other side of the room. It was sparsely furnished with a desk, a long table, and several old, dusty chairs.

Blake walked up to the table and reached out to touch it.

"Don't!" Quinn hissed.

"What?" Blake asked, jumping back.

"Look at all the dust on this stuff. If you touch that, your fingers will disturb the dust and leave evidence we can't get rid of. Someone's clearly coming down here every so often to check on the big computer things. We don't need to tip them off that we were here—especially since none of this furniture looks like it's been used in years."

Blake nodded. "Right. But how do they get down here?"

He shined his light around and found another tunnel opposite the door they entered in. They approached the archway that led to the tunnel and stopped to examine it with their flashlights. It was made of cinderblocks and not poured concrete like the one they had discovered that led them down into the chamber. About fifty paces away from them, a metal cage of some sort reflected back their light.

"Looks like the Batcave," Quinn said.

"What?" Blake asked.

"It looks like the elevator in the Batcave that goes up to Wayne Manor."

"Oh, right."

The boys made their way toward the other end of the tunnel. The cage, they discovered, separated them from a very old elevator shaft that disappeared into the darkness above them. Several chains hung on the far side of the shaft. Three vertical columns of steel I-beams—one on the back of the shaft and one on each side of the shaft, reinforced with cross bracing attached to the rock walls—supported what Quinn assumed was the elevator car frame. The inside of each I beam had gear teeth, so Quinn assumed the elevator car traveled by means of a geared mechanical system—maybe even a hand-crank.

A noise above him startled him.

"Turn your flashlight off," Quinn hissed, clicking his off. Blake complied.

Voices above them grew louder until the sudden screech of metal made both boys jump.

Someone opened the elevator door up there.

Footsteps on metal traveled down the shaft as men's voices echoed down with them. The metal screech echoed once more, and a mechanical device whirred to life, causing the chains on the back wall to shake. Suddenly, the tunnel and the control room behind them were bathed in white utility lights that switched on.

Quinn and Blake looked at each other, surprised.

"Run!" they both whispered.

Chapter 16

More Unanswered Questions

Blake

B lake pulled open the control room door and barely held it open for Quinn. He was almost across the chamber when he heard Quinn yelling at him in a loud whisper.

"Blake, stop!"

"Are you fucking kidding me?" Blake screeched, his lungs heaving for air as his flight response kicked in. He spun around to look at Quinn. "Where the hell are you?" he asked, alarmed that Quinn was not right behind him.

"I'm right here. I'm invisible."

Blake yelped and jumped back. "Oh my gosh, you really are. I can't see you!"

"That's the point. Oh look, you just disappeared!" Quinn exclaimed. "Dude! Now we're both invisible!"

"You're kidding," Blake said. He looked down at his hand. He was partially transparent, but the flashlight he held in his hand was floating in mid-air.

Quinn brought his flashlight close to Blake's hand. "Cool, huh?"

"I'm not fully invisible," Blake said.

"You are to me," Quinn confirmed. "I'm like, semi-see-through to myself, though."

"You're totally invisible to me."

"Wicked. I assume this must be how we can see ourselves when we're invisible to others or something. Weird how our clothes turned invisible, but the flashlights didn't. What are you feeling?"

"Maybe objects have to be concealed, in your pocket. I can't see your wallet, phone, or keys. I also can't see your backpack. Otherwise, I'm feeling...I'm surprised as hell there are other people here."

"Yeah, and our flashlights will be floating in midair if they see us."

"We have time," Blake said. "The elevator is still running."

"I was surprised, startled, maybe scared...less scared than surprised. Maybe being surprised has something to do with becoming invisible."

"This is fucking fantastic. I'm so going into the girls' locker room when we get back to school."

"Ew, dude. Gross," Quinn said. "Have a little respect."

"I'm kidding."

"No, you're not."

"You're right," Blake said, smiling. *I wonder if Quinn knows I'm smiling?*

"Come on, let's hide for a bit. If we leave, we'll learn nothing."

"Fine, but we're invisible, why do we need to hide?"

"Because I'm not sure we can control this power yet. Do you want to take that chance?"

"Good point. Where do we hide? All those lights turned on in the control room. There's no way they'll *not* see us in there."

"Down there," Quinn said, briefly shining his flashlight at the hatch that led to the battery room. "We can hide behind some of the batteries. There's plenty of room down there. Trust me."

After double-checking the hatch had no locking mechanism, the boys climbed down the ladder and hid behind two of the battery units. Above them, two men's voices echoed through the chamber, but they couldn't make out any of the words.

"My super hearing isn't working very well for some reason," Quinn whispered. "Try to focus on listening better or something."

"Okay," Blake whispered back.

He focused on the muffled words and tried to block out the faint buzz of the energy moving through the chamber floor above them.

"This isn't working," Blake whispered.

"Shut up, you only tried for like two seconds."

Blake exhaled in frustration and focused again. *Why isn't this working?*

The door screeched open and the voices became clear as the men entered the chamber. One of the men regaled the other about his latest sexual conquest.

"Gross," Quinn whispered.

"I'll check down here," the man with sexual bravado announced to his partner.

Shit.

Blake closed his eyes and tried to remember what being surprised felt like. The dull tapping of boots on the metal ladder signaled the man was descending into the battery room.

A moment later, Blake saw a flashlight beam swinging around the room.

"Nothing, all clear," the man said loudly, startling Blake. *If I wasn't invisible, I am now.*

The man climbed back up to the main chamber.

"Okay, let's go," a gruff voice in the chamber said. Blake heard him opening and closing the door that led to the tunnel the boys originally came through.

"Sucks, though, the batteries are still drained. Ever since that freak storm a couple weeks back."

"Yeah," the gruff man said, disinterested.

"Is it true all the orgone they'd been building up just disappeared? It's gonna take almost a year to stockpile all the energy they lost."

"Yup, it completely dissipated. Maybe if they had someone who knew how to use this stuff, we could all go home a lot sooner than watching them play rinky-dink-mad-scientist with this stuff. Besides, this place gives me the creeps."

"Meh, whatever. I think it's kind of cool, being able to manipulate the weather and all."

"That's just because you're smart enough to be more than a security guard to Victor; you're his computer nerd."

Oooh, these guys work for Victor and his mystery agency.

"Job security, my friend."

"Whatever," the gruff man said.

"At least, with the stuff upstairs. The old crap in the control room down here, I have no idea how that even works because—"

The control room door slammed shut and the men's voices became muffled once more.

Blake shined his flashlight to where Quinn was standing, but he saw nothing. "You there?"

"Yeah, I think have this invisibility thing down. Watch." A moment later, Quinn appeared. He waved at Blake, shielding his eyes from the bright light, and then disappeared.

Can I do that?

Blake shined the flashlight at—no, through—his hand.

Become visible!

Nothing.

"I'm still invisible. I can't control it yet. Shit."

"You will, don't worry. Let's get out of here."

"Right."

Blake led the way up the ladder and poked his head up before crawling all the way out. "It's clear," he whispered.

On the other side of the control room door, the machinery for the mysterious elevator at the end of the hall switched on.

"Wanna go back?" Blake asked, hoping Quinn would say no.

"I think I've seen enough. Let's get back to the car. I want to drive over to this museum and check things out on the surface. Besides, you heard the things those guys said…orgone energy, a freak storm, weather manipulation, and Victor. This is all tied together somehow. Oh, by the way, I can see you now," Quinn said as Blake pushed open the tunnel door.

Blake looked at his hand. *Become invisible! Boo! You're surprised!*

Nothing.

Dammit.

"All right, let's get out of here. I've had it with this place, too," Blake said, lying. Although he wanted to go back and explore, he agreed they needed to see what mysteries the museum grounds held. He led the way out, and Quinn followed him back in silence to the woods, where the bright, late-morning sunlight shone through the fading canopy of leaves.

"There it is," Blake said, pointing across the steering wheel at the simple sign welcoming guests to the museum.

"Sweet," Quinn said. "Now we need an inconspicuous place to park."

"Why not just pull in to the parking lot?"

Quinn chuckled. "Because the SUV has New Hampshire license plates, and two teenage boys walking in the front door of this rather unusual museum will surely raise someone's suspicions. Besides, I don't want to see Victor Kraze today, do you?"

"Nope," Blake answered, shaking his head. He saw a road coming up on the right. "Turn right, over there on Angel Point Road. If you park on the side of the road, we can walk back. Chances are anyone who works here is coming from the main road behind us and not wherever this goes."

"You're probably right," Quinn said, turning the car onto the dirt road.

Blake pulled out his cell phone and saw it still had no signal. "Dammit. I wanted to look up orgone energy, but I can't." He grabbed Quinn's phone from the center console. "Yours neither. Well, okay then, I guess we're going in blind."

"Don't worry," Quinn said, pulling over. "We'll search for it when we get home."

After they had parked, the boys walked back down the quiet road toward Orgonon, the name of the home-turned-museum of Wilhelm Reich.

"So, we're not gonna walk in through the front door, right?" Blake asked.

"Oh, hell no. We're gonna do what we do best around here…sneak through the woods." Quinn looked around and then winked at Blake. A second later he faded from view.

"Not fair. I can't turn invisible on demand yet. Besides, I thought we agreed not to use our powers up here?"

"That was in the cave. This is outside. Besides, you'd totally be invisible with me right now if you could."

"True."

"Look out!" Quinn yelled, his invisible hands grabbing Blake's shoulders.

"What?" he yelled, startled. He looked around and ducked slightly.

"There, remember this feeling. You just disappeared."

I'm feeling startled...surprised...shocked.

"We could walk to the front door now," Blake quipped.

"I don't know how long you can stay invisible. Better not chance it." Quinn slid his hand down Blake's arm and grabbed his wrist. Then, the boys left the road and cut into the woods, making their way toward the museum. Around them, bugs and chipmunks carried on with their lives, oblivious to the invisible teens traipsing through their woodland home.

Still invisible. This is freaking fantastic!

Several minutes later, they arrived at the edge of the woods and the start of a wide-open field between them and the museum. The field kept going, but they couldn't see beyond some trees that jutted out from the white museum building.

"Crap," Quinn said. "There's no way we can sneak up on the place from this direction."

Blake looked at his semi-transparent arm. He could feel Quinn's hand on his arm, but he couldn't see it. "I'm still invisible. I think we could run across the field and get to those woods behind the house. Or"—he pointed to a copse of trees a hundred yards away that provided better cover—"we could go over there and cut across the narrowest part of the field."

That was dumb, it's not like Quinn can see me pointing.

"Let's cut across here. We can always escape that way if we have to."

"Okay," Blake said, feeling the exhilaration of the moment surge in his veins. He double-checked his hand; it was still semi-transparent to him. "Let's go."

Quinn started, and Blake followed, staying connected to his friend. The boys ran across the field, their hearts pounding with anticipation and nervousness as they approached the tree line on the other side.

"Okay, now what?" Quinn asked.

"Try to stay invisible. Let's go behind the house and see if we can find whatever's on top of the underground chamber." They pressed deeper into the woods, the white museum behind them and to their left.

Fifteen minutes later, after passing several *No Trespassing* signs, Blake saw a glint of sunlight reflect on something metallic. "Over there," Blake said, pointing.

Stop pointing, he can't see you.

"Where?"

"Follow my lead," Blake said, leading Quinn toward the shiny object. They came to the edge of the tree line, stopped, and stared. In a wide-open area in front of them, to the right, three rows of ten or more gray bowl-shaped objects resembling satellite dishes extended far into the distance. To the left, a cluster of about fifty strange cannon-type devices pointed to the sky.

"Anti-aircraft guns?" Quinn asked.

"Out here?"

"Maybe they're left over from the war?"

"What war? This is Maine, not Europe."

"Good point."

Blake chuckled. Each cannon array contained ten long, narrow gray tubes arranged in two rows of five. Each array rested in black metal articulated frames cemented into the ground. Using what appeared to be hand cranks, the frames allowed the cannons to be swiveled and aimed. At the moment, all of the cannons pointed due west at a forty-five-degree upward angle.

"I know we keep joking about watching too much TV, but seriously, this is surreal. What in the hell are those things?" Blake asked. "Man, we're gonna have to scour the Internet about this place when we get home. I think we—"

"Shhh," Quinn uttered, squeezing Blake's arm. "Ten o'clock," he whispered.

A moment later, Blake's enhanced vision focused on two armed men in gray tactical garb exiting a metal door set in a flat-topped hexagonal concrete bunker the boys hadn't noticed yet. The metal door closed behind them and locked. The keypad on the door handle was the most advanced-looking piece of technology Blake had seen. The guards turned away and walked toward the far end of the open area.

A number of strange looking antennas mounted in steel and concrete pointed straight up. A particularly tall antenna at the center rose high into the sky, anchored by cables at three points along its length and the top that disappeared into the forest grounds.

"That's got to be where the underground chamber is," Quinn whispered. "Look at all that shit coming out of the ground."

"Those have to be the guards we heard in the chamber, unless there are more. I'd be willing to bet there are more than two guards here."

"Me too," Quinn agreed. "Except for the lack of fencing, this place seems pretty top secret to me."

"Wanna go check it out?" Blake asked.

"Eh," Quinn uttered. "Maybe we should just take some pictures with our phones."

"Dammit, why didn't we take pictures of the underground stuff?"

"Shit," Quinn exclaimed. "Well, let's take some now. Then I think I'm ready to go."

"Already?"

"Yeah. I can try to sneak around if you stay put, but if one of us becomes visible…"

He checked his arm again; it was still semi-transparent. "Yeah, yeah, I'll stay here just in case."

"Okay, be right back. I'll get as close as I can."

Blake felt Quinn let go of his hand. The sound of footsteps churning across the leafy and mossy woods reached his ears and then faded. He pulled out his phone, checked it was on silent, and snapped some photos. When he had finished, he put his phone back into his pocket and looked around, trying to use his enhanced vision. Other than the equipment in front of him, the natural woods surrounding everything seemed fine…until his eyes found a black wire suspended high in the trees above him.

He followed it with his eyes in one direction and saw it disappeared into the woods as it wrapped around the open area. He followed it in the other direction until he saw a security camera. *Aw crap. If there's one, there's more.*

He checked his arm again; it was solid, indicating he was no longer invisible.

"I can see you," Quinn whispered.

"Where are you?" Blake whispered back, using his super hearing to listen to Quinn.

"Next to the bunker."

Blake looked over but didn't see his friend. "At least you're still invisible."

"You can do it, I have faith in you."

"Okay, fine, but whatever you do, stay invisible. There's a security camera above me pointing at you."

"Oooh, okay. I'm almost done. Then we can go."

Blake looked at his arm and focused. A moment later, it became semi-transparent. *Yes! Another power I can control.*

A minute or two later, Blake heard Quinn trudging toward him. "Okay, let's go, I'm finished," Quinn said.

"Race you back to the SUV?" Blake asked.

"Invisible racing? You're on. Just don't trip over me!" Then the boys ran back to the SUV. Blake felt victorious because he remained invisible for the duration of the race.

When the boys arrived back in Portsmouth, Quinn parked Dad's SUV in the garage at five o'clock, and Blake followed him into the house.

On the kitchen counter, Quinn found a note scrawled in Daddio's handwriting:

Hi Q! Forgot to remind you we're at Dad's office-charity event thing tonight, probably won't be back until 10:00. Made you some empanadas for dinner, they're in the fridge.

Love you,

Daddio

PS—if you're going to play hooky from school with Blake, let us know, okay? I don't like getting automated calls from the school noting your absence. Don't let it happen again or there will be consequences.

Quinn swallowed nervously and chuckled, relieved he'd received a pass.

"This your first time cutting school?" Blake asked.

"Of course," Quinn responded. "I'm gonna make them a promise not to do that again."

The boys headed upstairs to Quinn's bedroom. They sat next to each other at his desk and researched orgone energy and the Orgonon home-turned-museum on his laptop, reading whatever they could find on the obscure science. Unfortunately, the Internet only provided limited information that seemed to fall off shortly after Dr. Reich's death. Whatever was going on in the underground facility in Rangeley had either been eliminated or hidden from the general public and the Internet.

"I give up," Quinn said, pushing his laptop away. "Unless something changes, we're not going to know what happened to us. We're going to keep getting powers, and the only person who can help us is Mr. St. Germain. Otherwise, we'd have to reach out to Victor Kraze, and as long as we're not dying, I see no reason to speak with that man."

Blake nodded, and his stomach growled. *But he'd have the answers we need...if you won't talk with him, maybe I should figure out how to connect with him...maybe a simple phone call would suffice...*

Quinn poked Blake's noisy stomach. "Let's eat. I'm starving, too. Want to eat those empanadas?"

"Yes, definitely."

Chapter 17

With Us or Against Us

Blake

B lake finished wiping down the counter and rinsed his rag in the sink. A lull in customers afforded him an opportunity to clean up, knowing the after-work commuter demand for coffee was right around the corner. The front door to the coffee shop opened behind him, and he quickly glanced at the door.

"Be right with you," he said.

"Take your time," a familiar voice said.

Blake's eyes popped open in surprise. He froze as his mind put together the voice that spoke with the face he'd glanced at a moment ago.

Oh shit.

Blake spun around and stared into the familiar eyes of the man in the black suit.

"Hello, Blake," the man said.

"Hello, Victor," Blake responded. "What brings you to Portsmouth?" *How did you know I wanted to talk with you? Or is this mere coincidence?*

Victor scanned the menu and smiled. "Earl Grey tea, hot."

Blake smirked. "This isn't Star Trek."

Victor tilted his head and smiled back. "No, it's not, but I still like Earl Grey tea, and I'd like a cup of it, please."

Blake didn't move. "You came all the way to Portsmouth for a cup of tea?"

Victor took a deep breath and smiled again. "Of course not. I came to speak with you. I'd like my tea to go, please."

Blake nodded. "I can't talk right now. I'm working."

Victor nodded at him. "Don't worry, I know you're busy right now. Perhaps we could talk later? How about we meet in Prescott Park fifteen minutes after your shift ends. It's a public place, there will be people around, and you will have nothing to worry about. I only want to talk."

"Fine," Blake said.

"Great," Victor responded. "Look for me on one of the public wooden piers."

Blake nodded and turned around to prepare Victor's tea. At the same time, his boss came out and started tinkering at the register.

Good, I won't be alone in here with my back to Victor.

When Blake finished pouring the hot water, he dropped the Earl Grey tea bags into the paper to-go cup and fastened the lid. Then, he turned around and handed it to Victor.

"Two fifty," Blake said.

Victor smiled and passed him a five-dollar bill.

"Keep the change," Victor said. "See you at the park." Then he took his tea cup and walked out of the cafe.

Blake clocked out and headed for his bike. He pulled on his helmet and rolled the bike out the back door of the coffee shop. Then he peddled his way down Daniel Street against traffic and made his way over to Prescott Park. He spotted Victor's black suit on the first pier, the pier he had seen Quinn waiting at. This time, however, Quinn wasn't around.

Since Blake was early, he rode through the park, scanning its guests and visitors. Only two people stood out as odd to him. Each wore sunglasses, dark jeans, a polo shirt, and was reading a book. One was in direct line of sight with the pier. The other was situated in the middle of the park but still within line of sight with the pier.

Those must be his bodyguards or his henchmen.

Blake turned around and peddled to the pier. When he arrived, he hopped off and walked his bike to the lookout.

Victor turned around and smiled. "Hello again, Blake," he said.

Blake nodded. "Victor." When he arrived at the lookout area, he rested his bike against the wooden railing. Then he faced the water and stared across it with Victor.

"This never gets old," Victor said. "It's not the beach, but the harbor is beautiful, despite all the machinery over there." He pointed at the shipyard.

Blake nodded, silently agreeing with the man. *I couldn't agree more, but the shipyard is part of the charm here.*

"That castle thing over there is pretty cool too," Victor added, pointing to the far end of the shipyard. "Do you know what it is?"

"Sure, it's the abandoned naval prison. Too much asbestos or something to tear it down."

"Ah. Too bad, it would make a really cool hotel."

"What do you want, Victor?" Blake asked. "You didn't come down here to comment on local scenery or check up on me."

"Actually, I did come to check on you. Occasionally, strange things happen in Rangeley, and it's my job to make sure the people who are affected by those strange things are okay. Are you okay?"

Blake looked at him, his brows furled in confusion. "Yes, I'm okay. Is that all?"

"Of course not," Victor answered.

"Then what do you want?" Blake snapped, unsure of whether he wanted to continue this conversation or walk away. His desire to succeed where Quinn had given up motivated him to stay with Victor. *Don't be a fool, this is my chance to learn everything.*

"Blake, I believe you and I have similar ambitions," Victor said. "I can usually tell when someone shares my unique ideology."

"Your what?" Blake said.

Victor smiled. "In other words, we think a lot alike. Specifically, your brand of justice matches mine to a T."

How do you know that? Have you been spying on me? Do you know about the guys I burned? Blake hesitated to answer, unsure of what to say. He swallowed away his nervousness. "Go on."

"The world is full of good people and bad people. Do you know what the problem with bad people is?" Victor asked, still staring out at the water.

"They do bad things," Blake answered sarcastically.

Victor nodded. "Something like that. However, the world is not full of evil villains, Blake. The world is full of people with…unique perspectives."

I'm listening, but what the hell are you talking about?

Victor smiled again, turning to face Blake. "I can tell by your face I've confused you. What I mean is, nobody wakes up in the morning and says, 'I'm going to do evil things today.' Nobody sits around their kitchen table and plots out the next evil scheme or the next evil thing they could do; life isn't a movie. In reality, people make choices others regard as morally correct or morally reprehensible."

"Okay," Blake said, clearing his throat and the awkwardness he heard in his voice.

"It's easy when you think about it in terms of comic books," Victor said. "You like comic books, right?"

"Yes," Blake stammered. *How the hell did you know that?*

"Take Batman. He's a good guy, and most people regard him as the superhero who regularly fights evil enemies like the Joker, Two-face, or the Riddler. Those kinds of villains are made up, but they paint a picture of what most people think of when they think of bad or evil people, right?"

Blake nodded and turned, leaning his hip on the railing.

"In the world we live in, there is no Joker, Two-face, or Riddler, right?" Victor extended a hand to Blake, waiting for him to agree.

"I follow you," Blake said.

"Take Saddam Hussein. Take Hitler. Intensely evil and villainous figures of history who committed atrocities in the name of…" Victor extended his hand again and waited for Blake to finish his sentence.

Blake shrugged. "Doing evil?"

"No," Victor said. "Doing what they thought was right but the world found morally reprehensible. I guarantee that when those men and others like them woke up in the morning, the first question they did not ask themselves was 'What evil thing can I do today?' They woke up in the morning, had breakfast just like you and me, and then set out to figure out how they could accomplish the next step of their plan."

"Are you trying to tell me those were good men?" Blake asked, suddenly feeling very skeptical of Victor. *Maybe this is what Quinn is worried about.*

Victor shook his head vehemently. "Absolutely not. In their twisted intentions, those men committed evil atrocities that go beyond the pale. They committed acts of violence, murder, genocide, and other unspeakable things against humanity, and they needed to be punished. I think we agree on this point, do we not?"

Blake nodded. "We do."

"Good." Victor leaned on the railing and studied Blake for a moment. "What if I told you there was an organization that sought to punish so-called *evil doers* when governments like that of the United States failed to intervene or act responsibly for the moral good of the planet."

"I would say that's a pretty awesome organization," Blake answered. "Why?"

"Imagine an organization that found people who got away with murder, who got away with rape, or worse, got away with crimes against humanity on a massive or global scale. An autonomous organization that acted in the best interest of humanity and did whatever it took to make sure the men, women, and groups who committed those crimes received swift justice, the kind our American judicial system refuses to prescribe for such...criminals."

Blake took a moment to process Victor's words. He thought of the two men he'd dealt with on Four Tree Island who'd threatened the girls. He remembered the powerful feeling of satisfaction and justice he experienced when he burned them. *That must be what Victor is talking about, stopping the criminals and making them pay...which is exactly what I want to do with my powers.*

"You've got my attention," Blake said.

"Good," Victor said, smiling. "I knew we'd see eye to eye on this."

Blake turned back to the churning water of the Piscataqua River and rested his elbows on the railing. "You still haven't told me what this has to do with me."

"Ah," Victor said, "yes, let's get to that part." Victor also turned to the water and rested his elbows on the wooden railing. "How have you been feeling since you left Rangeley?" he asked.

Blake looked at him for a moment and then brought his eyes back to the river water. "I told you, I feel fine."

"You haven't felt anything unusual?" Victor asked.

"Was I supposed to?" Blake answered.

"I would think so," Victor said flatly.

Holy shit, does he know? Does he know about our powers? Is he trying to recruit me into some weird army he controls?

"I like to think I'm a bit of a talent scout," Victor continued. "When I see talent and potential, I go after it. One day, perhaps, you may join our organization and become a powerful asset."

"An asset?" Blake said, the disgust clear in his voice.

Victor smirked. "I'm sorry, I know *asset* sounds cold, harsh, and very military-like. Our agents are people, not disposable things. When someone agrees with our philosophy, we take a particular interest in mentoring that person and shaping their mind so they can help us execute justice where others often fail."

Blake chuckled. "That sounds like a fancy way to say you want to brainwash me into serving you."

Victor laughed, surprising Blake. "Brainwashing you would serve no purpose," Victor said, his tone changing and becoming serious. "You have a mind with potential, and it is a mind waiting to grow and be shaped. Others with limited minds only see two steps in front of themselves, and they need…stronger conditioning…because they don't understand how they should behave or think. You already think like us, and we want to help you grow."

"When?" Blake asked.

"As soon as possible," Victor answered.

"Well, I have two more years of high school to complete, and then I'm supposed to go to college, but—"

"You can still do those things," Victor said. "In fact, it's best that you do those very normal things that will not look suspicious to anyone else."

He's talking about Quinn.

Blake stared at Victor. "Am I alone in this little adventure quest of yours? Or are you talking to someone else?"

Victor smiled. "You're alone in this."

"I see," Blake answered. *He doesn't want Quinn involved…which is probably for the best because Quinn wouldn't fit in here. He wouldn't agree with this kind of justice.*

"It's not that we don't want to include your best friend," Victor said, his voice tentative, "but we do not believe Quinn appreciates our point of view." Victor paused, leaving his sentence hanging in the air for Blake to pick up.

Blake nodded. "You're right. Quinn doesn't think like us. All he wants to do is round up the criminals and let the justice system deal with them."

"Round up the criminals?" Victor asked, smiling. "Does he want to be a police officer?"

Shit.

Blake realized Victor had set him up and he had almost revealed their super-power status to Victor.

You can fix this.

"No," Blake answered. "But we do read a lot of comics and we often talk about superheroes and super villains, so I know what Quinn would do."

"I see," Victor said, smiling. "Would you be comfortable keeping this little secret from Quinn?" Victor asked. "The organization I work for, that you could work for, doesn't exist as far as anyone else is concerned. In fact, if you turn my offer down, I'll have to make sure you realize we don't exist."

"Is that a threat?" Blake asked.

"Of course not," Victor answered, chuckling. "Just a reality, something I need to protect. Basically, we would part ways and you would never see me again."

"Even if we went camping in Rangeley again?" Blake asked sarcastically.

Victor met his sarcasm with a smile. "I can't predict the future, Blake. But I can predict you will be a strong asset to this organization. You will help us become more powerful than ever before."

Oh my gosh, he knows. He knows we have powers. Don't say anything, make him say it first. Don't volunteer this shit.

"However," Victor said, "I don't think this will be a problem. I think you're looking for a real opportunity to make a difference in the world, something you may not be able to do today, but something you can do with time as you learn. I'm willing to help mentor you, and I have a great team of individuals who can help you as well. Think about this offer carefully, Blake. We know your parents are less than supportive, and we would take care of *everything* for you."

"But not Quinn?" Blake asked flatly.

"No," Victor answered, shaking his head. "At least, not yet. Don't get me wrong, Quinn's heart is in the right place—like so many other people who believe in the justice systems of the world's dominant governments. But in reality, there are always people who slip through the cracks. Those are the folks we go after."

"How come I never hear about this on the news?" Blake asked.

"Simple. It takes a lot of skillful planning and methodical execution. Besides, an autonomous organization like ours would attract unwanted attention and become a public spectacle if it were discovered. That's why we keep a low profile and select our members carefully. You'll be screened. My invitation does not guarantee you a spot."

"But if I say no," Blake answered, "you'll do what?"

"We'll part ways, and I'll see to it you never remember me."

"That still sounds like a threat."

"It's not, I promise. We won't hurt you."

"What are you going to do? Wipe my memory like *Men in Black?*" Blake asked.

"Something like that," Victor said. When his face didn't move, Blake knew the man wasn't kidding.

"And Quinn won't get hurt?" Blake asked.

"Of course not," Victor said. "Why would he get hurt? Is he a criminal mastermind that needs to be brought to justice?"

Blake laughed. "No, of course not."

"All right then. Quinn will be safe."

Blake nodded. "Okay, I'm in. I'll think about it for a few days, but I don't think I'll change my mind."

"That's excellent news," Victor said.

"How will I contact you?" Blake asked.

"You won't. I'll contact you," Victor said.

"That doesn't sound ominous or anything."

Victor chuckled. "I suppose it does. Just remember I have a lot to protect, so it's in my best interest to only share the information you need. Okay?"

Blake nodded. "Okay."

"Have a great rest of the day," Victor said, extending his hand to Blake. They shook hands, and then Victor walked back to Prescott Park.

Blake turned and rested his backside on the railing. The two plainclothes security guards were still there, and when Victor walked past, they closed their books and followed him.

He smiled as a feeling of satisfaction grew inside him. *I knew Victor would have the answers I needed, and as it turns out, this little chat was exactly what I needed. Now I have the chance to learn more about what happened to us and what I can do with my powers while Quinn is playing the hero. I just hope he comes around and joins us...soon.*

The End of this Book

Guardians continues with...

Book 2: Unidentified Phenomenon

The manhunt is on…

…but no one knows who—or what—to look for.

Impossibly heroic superhuman saves, wanted criminals vanishing into thin air, and thugs washing up with unexplainable third-degree burns can mean only one thing: someone has taken the law into their own hands.

But who? And why?

With the Department of Homeland Security breathing down the necks of city officials, Quinn and Blake must hide their superpowers from everyone, even their families.

Time is running out.

How long can they outrun the growing pile of damning evidence against them?

UNIDENTIFIED PHENOMENON is the second book of The Guardian Series
and is part of the Spekter Superhero Universe.

Get it now!

Before you go...

Please Leave a Review

The world needs to know how you feel about this book. Don't let them down. Leave an online review wherever you bought this book or on Goodreads today.

Subscribe to My Newsletter

Want to learn about my newest releases before anyone else? Then subscribe to my newsletter by scanning the QR code below with your smartphone's camera. I promise not to spam you! Your readership is too important to me.

Damien Benoit-Ledoux Books

Online Bonus Content

Explore the Spekter Superhero Universe Online!

The Spekter Superhero Universe is a fantastic superhero universe that contains several published or in-process novels bout amazing superheroes and deadly super villains. I carefully designed the website to support the series universe by providing all kinds of background information about the characters and the places of their world that I couldn't include in the novels. I hope you enjoy what you discover here, and happy reading!

worldanvil.com/w/the-spekter-superhero-universe-damientronus

I can also be found online at the following social media sites:

- Patreon: patreon.com/damientronus

- Twitter: twitter.com/damientronus

- Goodreads: goodreads.com/damientronus

- Instagram: instagram.com/spektersuperheroes

Acknowledgments

My husband and handsome hero, Tim, for his constant encouragement and willingness to share in this part of my life. I truly appreciate your support as I jockey between our lives, work, and several novels. I love you, through all of time and space…

Transcriptionist

My amazing sister-in-law, Joanna Ledoux, took audio recordings of chapters and scenes from long drives I made and diligently transcribed them for me, saving me hours of work.

Editing

My husband, Tim.

Proofreading

Alexandra Ellis – rabbitrune.wordpress.com

Cover Design

Miblart

Beta Readers

My team of beta readers who pre-read the novel and provided feedback and suggestions to strengthen the story. Thank you.

- Victor Freeman

- Gea Kuil

Contributors

These fine superhero supporters added something to the story, such as an idea, a character, subject matter expertise, or simply shared their thoughts with me about something I was working on.

- Andrew Rowe

- Ron St. Germain

About the Author

Damien's mind is a magical and nerdy place where fantastic heroes defend amazing worlds from dangerous villains who run amuck in an epic struggle to take over the universe. Recently, the brightest and best from this colorful cast of characters have made their way into notes, plots, stories, and novels for you to read and enjoy.

Damien strongly believes the real world we live in should be a place where LGBTQA equality and acceptance are second nature and never questioned.

When he's not working or spending time with his husband and their dog, Damien weaves this philosophy into the exciting lives of his characters and the fantastic space battles and romances they endure so they'll stop taking over his dreams at night.

And finally, he wants you to remember a very important thing:

No matter how bad your day is at work, it's always important to be grateful that you don't work for a Sith Lord.

Made in United States
Troutdale, OR
08/17/2024

22091684R00116